i

c

o

p

e

For more information, find CCM at:

http://copingmechanisms.net

THE 2015 CCM COMPENDIUM

XTX BRANDI WELLS ANDREA KNEELAND JAYINEE BASU SEAN H DOYLE KATIE JEAN SHINKLE M KITCHELL DARBY LARSON JOHN COLASACCO JAMIE IREDELL BRANDON HOBSON MARK KATZMAN BEN BROOKS RYAN W BRADLEY KIRSTEN ALENE BRIAN OLIU COREY ZELLER EVAN RETZER

CONTENTS

THE 2015 CCM CATALOGUE

SELECTIONS FROM THE 2016 CATALOGUE

TODAY I AM A LION

| xTx

Today I am a lion. My little brother is a lion. We are lions together. We roam the woods behind our house until our footpads bleed. Lots of hunting but also playing and sleeping. There are mostly squirrels so we have to hunt a LOT because our stomachs are so big and the squirrels are so small. Once in a while there is a bunny or a raccoon. Not much heartier. I turn back into a boy to shoot them with my BB gun. Each time I kill one, my brother roars. I become a lion again and we go rip it apart with our teeth. Blood smears our chins, our short manes.

Our mother's favorite color is roses. When I was the only cub, they were everywhere. All around the yard. I'd pet their petals with my paws, lost in their scent. "Why are there so many, mommy?" "Because they're my favorite color," she'd say. Then she'd chase me all around the roses, pouncing and pouncing until she'd catch me. Her paws so giant they'd eat up my chest. I had nowhere else to go but my back against the grass. My growls turned into that of a boy's laughter and hers into a mother's. When we both tired, she'd pick me up by my scruff, her fierce mouth soft against my fur, and carry me into our den where we'd curl together and nap until our father came home from his hunting. His muzzle dried bloody from the kill, carcass heavy and dragging.

My little brother doesn't know our mother's favorite color. The roses all died after our father didn't come back from the hunt. He'd been in her belly the entire time and never was able to see them.

"But what about when she'd roar?" I asked, "Couldn't you see then?"

"No. I was sleeping."

"How did you sleep with so much roaring?" I asked. My mother's roars were deafening. I remember putting my head into my paws to drown it out.

After our father didn't come back my mother couldn't stop roaring. It was all she did. That's when our play ended. That's when our den went rotten. That's when the roses died. I tried to save them at first. I gathered their mottled bodies from the ground with my boy hands and brought them to her, hoping it would stop her roars.

I stood inside her hot breath, inside the bottomless sound that kept pushing out of her. "Look mommy, your favorite color!"

It took many times to make myself heard. When she finally ceased her roar I felt a hope spark inside of me. We stood there together for a minute in the new silence her roar had left. The den fell away and our house stepped forward. I could see the squashed couch again. The carpet with all the rips and spills. I could even smell the awful from the kitchen. It felt like a waking up. All of a sudden, I didn't want it. I wanted to push it back. But it was too late.

I could see her face want to change for a minute. Her fur thinned to skin and back. Her eyes blurred between gold and blue. Her muzzle retracted then lengthened, teeth sabered then squared, ears sliding from the top of her head down the sides and then returning. The two parts of her fighting for what world she wanted to belong to.

She never came back.

My brother and I walk both worlds. We have to. Our mother is stuck as a lion and we are lions but we are also boys. We still need the things of man.

Ever since my brother was a cub I've had to teach him the ways of both livings. I start him early on the hunt. Earlier than even I had as now we are our only hunters. His approaches are rough at first and he is scared and timid, but as he ages he learns and we triumph together as young lions. As brothers. He fights to be the one to bring home the kill to our mother. I know he just wants a chance for her to see him—he never played with her through the roses, never felt her paws collapsing his chest. I fight him back but let him win every time. I already know what it's like to be seen.

The ways of man take up most of our days. I show him all of the things to keep his body well, how to cover its weakness in clothing to stay warm, how to feed it with things no lion would ever touch, and I bring him to school where he resists, "Let's go home. Let's be lions!" I shush him and explain, "Learn all the things they teach you so you can be free to be a lion. Like mother did, like father did." The mention of "father" always quiets him. It's a tool that hurts but I use it often because it's hard raising a cub that isn't yours. It's hard being everything for everyone when you just want to be someone else's everything.

At night we go to sleep as lions. Lions, but still cubs.

We join our mother in her part of the den. She is so massive. She is the biggest thing in our lives.

We curl up next to her warmth which is all she has left to give.

SELECTIONS FROM *"THIS BORING APOCALYPSE"*
| BRANDI WELLS

She is gone long hours and I worry she is seeing someone else so I cut off her arms

Without arms she cannot drag herself to work. Without arms she cannot drag herself anywhere. We will stay here together in the house we've grown accustomed to with its floral couch and claw foot tub. We have made a home for ourselves and she will respect that.

Sometimes when I tire of looking at her, I take her outside and leave on her on the front porch. She is quiet and watches birds and squirrels climb up tree trunks.

I sit inside with the legs, tracing my mouth over flesh and pulling them to my body, warming the skin with my skin. I only bring her back inside when it gets dark.

Even with these breaks, I tire of her lounging around the house, always in the way, always underfoot.

I wish you would do something, I say, but she doesn't answer. *You can still roll,* I say. *You are acting pitiful for no reason. Obviously you can roll. I have seen you roll.* I pick her up and carry her out into the street. *There,* I say. *Roll away.* I push her with my foot, a light kick, just enough to get her started.

She rolls but has trouble keeping herself straight. She veers off into the ditch and I have to put her into the middle of the road over and over. Eventually she quits rolling and just closes her eyes.

Okay, I say. *We'll go back inside.*

She grows less beautiful

It is hard to look at her. Her legs and arms were once strong and firm and expendable. I worry about her expendable parts now. How many are left? What can she survive without? I worry I won't possess the skill to make the necessary cuts. I worry how long it will take to whittle her down to the smallest viable version of herself and what will be left then? Will I even like what's left?

Her appendix seems an easy choice. *You do not need it,* I tell her, gouging it out with clean deep cuts. She twists and turns, but the appendix comes out easily. It glistens, hardly drips. I toss her into a bathtub of ice and she cringes but can go nowhere. I try to leave her to herself, but I use some of the ice to make myself margaritas on the rocks. She used to love margaritas on the rocks.

Do you remember? I ask, *how you loved margaritas on the rocks?*

She doesn't remember.

Do you remember? I ask, *the time you peed down the side of my car, telling me that you could pee standing up?*

But she doesn't answer. Only shivers and closes her eyes.

With all her shivering there can be hardly any peace at all. *Quiet,* I tell her, but from the bathroom there's a constant rattling noise. I hear it in the hallway, the kitchen, the living room and even in the front yard. I can't enjoy meals. Every time I try to take a bite, rattle. Rattle. Rattle. Rattle. I eat loud foods. Celery sticks and carrots. Potato chips. But these foods are not loud enough to mask her noise.

In the mornings I take her outside to lie in the sun and feel warm

I lay her in the sunniest part of the yard. I rub her body with suntan lotion and place mirrors all around her torso, so the sun cooks her.

Are you going to eat me? she asks.

I hold her up to the sun and look at her body. I imagine sandwiches and stew and porridge and breakfast burritos and I look at her leathered, crinkling skin.

No, I say. *I do not think I can eat you.*

I gather slender people and cook them in the sun.

Shhh, I tell the slender people, *shhhh.*

But it is hard for them to listen because I have cracked their skulls open delightfully.

You are delightful, I tell them.

They cook and cook until their bodies are delicious brown leather that I cover with garlic and cracked black pepper and olive oil. I take their small bodies inside to share with her, but she tells me, *NO*, she does not like olive oil.

To impress her I tan my body and it is so tan, so brown, so cracked and leathery. But she is not impressed. She will not open her eyes when I stand over her tub of ice water. She won't even shiver. She won't give me the satisfaction of a shiver and her shivers are so satisfying. I can subsist off only shivers for whole years of my life. In fact, for the first seventeen years of our relationship, I did.

To spite her I practice being beautiful

I hold it for one minute. I am beautiful for one minute. Then I try five minutes. Ten minutes. Half an hour. After a few weeks I am beautiful for hours at a time. Eventually I am beautiful for days. I can be beautiful in my sleep. I lie beside her ice tub to show her and she shouts, attempting to wake me every few hours to assure me that, *YES*, I am still beautiful and she is still watching me and no not for a moment was I ever not beautiful.

THE DIFFERENCE BETWEEN
| ANDREA KNEELAND

I realize with certainty that my husband is an asshole about three years into the marriage, while I am delirious with a flu-borne fever, freezing beneath cold yellow sweated-through bed sheets, bones shaking like caged mice. Instead of going to the store to get me NyQuil, he forces my legs into the harness of a strap-on, sits on top of me and fucks himself while I try not to die.

~

I never file any divorce papers. I leave him all of my underwear because he likes to wear them so much. I leave him all of my everything because I am afraid of confrontation. I write him an email, withdraw all of our savings, buy a white 1987 Acura. I buy some new bumper stickers to cover up the previous owner's bumpers stickers. I drive about 90 miles away. I buy some used clothes. I find a room and roommates. I find an administrative job with a wine importer. I go to art galleries and dive bars and tell people I work for a wine importer and I am impressed with myself for living in the world alone.

~

I sit on the rooftop and eat marijuana truffles with my college-age roommate. We talk about getting matching tattoos. It's dusking across the city and the skyline is melting into a dirty-looking night. Beneath the chocolate, the pot is candied like ginger and is stronger than we thought it would be. We knew better than to buy weed candy from a stranger in the Mission, but we did it anyway. We should have split the truffles in half. We should have split the truffles in quarters. We are stuck on the roof because we cannot move. When it is pitch black, I can still see the skyscrapers in the distance. I can see the Bay Bridge, even though the view from my rooftop never features the Bay Bridge. I can see everything, and it's beautiful.

My body floats through the blacklessness and I listen to voices carry through the air like birds, like the bodiless bodies of feathered strangers. The voices are birds without bodies. They are people without birds. Something has become confused. Something has become confused and I am spinning but everything is joyous and I realize that I am only spinning because I have escaped. I feel a great and indescribable love for my car. *My car is a bird*, I say and silence responds. *My car is a bird*, I say. Nobody knows that I'm married except for people who don't exist anymore. My body is a broken anchor made of bones. I sink beneath the skin of the rooftop. The air is a blanket of ice. I think that maybe I am happy.

Another roommate comes up to the roof to talk to us. She is drunk on free wine I brought home from work. She is telling us a story I don't understand. *The first time I met him he was wearing a Mickey Mouse watch and he gave me drugs, so I knew I'd never be his friend, she tells us. He was the first person I slept with here. No, wait, the second. It doesn't matter.* I fade way from her voice. Everyone I've met in this city is from somewhere else. She stays with us until it is too cold to breathe and then climbs back down on the slippery metal of the ladder and leaves the two of us helpless. This is what it means to be happy. We fall asleep and I wake up with numb toes, wondering at the beauty of the world and the luck of my life and the difference between now and then. In the morning, I walk to my car and I learn that if you do not curb your wheels on a 3% grade, the city will ticket you. I draw a bird in the center of my steering wheel.

~

The wine importer goes out of business. I sell my car. I don't pay the ticket. I sit in my room and touch dozens of bottles of Argentine wine and think about what nice severance gifts they are. I eat white rice with salt for dinner. I pet strangers' dogs on the street. I open a bottle of wine. I collect unemployment. I watch YouTube videos with my roommates. I eat Top Ramen for dinner. I drink more wine.

~

I go to the park with the youngest roommate and we spread a worn sheet across the grass. I close my eyes and listen as she reads to me from Vanity Fair.

When I open my eyes, I see a woman dressed like a pony. She is dressed in black straps of leather, high black boots, black gloves, black bit and bridle, black leather mask with horse ears. Her dyed black hair is pulled tight into a tight black braid, and a tight black braid of tight human hair swings behind her ass. She is pulling a rickshaw. The rickshaw rides two men, each holding half of her reins. One of them smokes a cigar.

I nudge my roommate away from her reading. Everyone in the park stares. *There are children around*, I say to my roommate. There are children around, and my roommate tells me that I'm a prude and *that there is nothing wrong with someone expressing their sexuality* and I begin to laugh, and then I realize that she's serious. I am reminded again that she's ten years younger than me and she's from Ohio and she's taking an undergrad Human Sexuality class this semester and she doesn't know any better. This suddenly seems insurmountable.

There is a difference between a fetish and an all-consuming obsession, I tell her. *That woman's life is ruined*, I tell her, but then, ten minutes later, the woman walks by again, pulling a different pair of people in the rickshaw. Two women: one with a sunhat and one with a parasol, both laughing about something. I can't imagine how hot she must feel beneath the mask. I can't imagine how her feet must hurt. *There she is again*, I tell my roommate and we watch together.

The third time the ponygirl walks by, pulling two teenage boys, my roommate doesn't even look. She is still angry with me for saying that the woman's life is ruined. *Maybe she charges for the rides*, I say. *Maybe this is how she makes a living*, I say, and I start to feel hopeful. I start to think that the woman is maybe a genius. *Maybe she does it for free*, my roommate says. *For anyone who asks.* This is sadder than anything else that I could have imagined.

I spend the rest of the day online trying to find out about the rickshaw ponygirl at Golden Gate Park. I find nothing and this makes me feel even worse.

~

I steal my roommate's underwear. I forget why I thought anything about architecture against sky. I open a bottle of wine. I sit on the roof alone. I eat discount lunchmeat that looks like worn down pieces of carpet. I sit in my roommate's bed and try to smoke ash from her pipe. I collect unemployment. I can't afford a tattoo. I drink more wine. I collect unemployment.

~

After four months of joblessness, I get my first call for an interview. I stand in Kinko's thinking unkind thoughts about my husband. I am watching a woman make hundreds of copies of a missing dog flyer. She is alone, crying on the Xerox machine. I don't even need to make any copies. I just want to use the stapler.

The stapler is chained to a table next to the crying woman. I'm afraid that if I approach the stapler, the woman will ask me if I've seen her dog and I'll tell her that it's probably dead.

I move away from the woman and the fliers and the stapler and I study the dirtied carpet, searching for a fallen paperclip, which I guess would be an okay substitution for a stapler. I'm not picky. There is no difference between a stapler and a paperclip. I don't see the difference between substitutions or synonyms or buses and cars or cats and dogs or recessions and depressions or any of the other things that other people think are different.

I try to remember if life has always been like this: a series of in-comprehensible obstacles blocking the most minor goals. I can't re-member. There are no paperclips on the floor. I consider going to the job interview without a staple or a paperclip, but handing in loose sheets of paper seems like such a bad first impression. You have to be careful with first impressions. Like that woman at the copy machine or the ponygirl at the park; I'll never be their friend.

I walk next door to the Chinese restaurant and ask them if they have a stapler, but they don't speak English so I don't get what I want. I sit down and order a bowl of hot and sour soup. When they bring the soup, I let it drip all over my resume and references while I think more unkind thoughts about my husband. I watch the clock on the wall for a while before I realize that it's broken. Outside on the corner, a homeless man plays the saxophone for a boy with Down syndrome, who claps and dances to the music. The Down syndrome boy's parents stand nearby, looking on. I wonder if the parents will give the saxophone player any money. I go home and open a bottle of wine.

~

I pick up the phone and talk to my mother. I spend more time not explaining to her the details of why I left my husband. I wonder how to explain a thing like that, the breaking point, the point of realization, to my mother or my father, or to any of the other ghosts who used to be part of my life. I wonder if the ponygirl speaks to her parents. I wonder if the woman at Kinko's speaks to her parents. I wonder if the man with the saxophone speaks to his parents. I wonder how they all became so alone in the world. I drink the last bottle of wine. I wonder if I am alone in the world. I do not pick up the phone the next time my mother calls. Or the next time. Or the next time. I ignore emails from my husband. I ignore emails from prospective employers. I ignore the footsteps of my roommates. I google "Golden Gate Park ponygirl." I eat McDonald's for dinner. I stop paying my cell phone bill. I don't miss having a phone. I set up a Google alert for "Golden Gate Park ponygirl."

~

I don't want to waste the whole afternoon. I want to be able to say that I've done something with my day. I stuff all of my clothes into one washing machine. I can barely close the door. The instructions on the machine specifically prohibit what I'm doing. But I have a plan and that plan includes washing two loads of laundry in one machine.

A crazy man walks into the laundromat just after I press start and he ruins the rest of my plan, which had consisted of walking to the drugstore up the street and reading all of the gossip magazines. In my plan, while I read the gossip magazines I do not think about anything but celebrity fashion and diet tips. I don't recognize most of the celebrities in the magazines because I don't have a TV, but they are gorgeous and interesting strangers.

The man is unwashed. He clicks his jaw and points at me, then drops his arms. His paws clench themselves tight like a stroke victim's, and he walks in a tiny circle. I stare at the floor. I stare at the ceiling. I look everywhere but his face. I can't leave now.

He is the kind of crazy person who steals clothes and sells them. It's warm enough today. He can take my clothes to the park and lay them out and they'll dry in a few hours and then he'll take them to the Tenderloin and sell them for 50 cents apiece.

I understand that leaving my clothes unattended was a risky venture in the first place, but I could have taken the risk had the potential for stolen clothes been only theoretical. Now that I am faced with what I am sure is a certainty, I can't walk away.

I scoot my plastic chair across the linoleum, as close to the washing machine as I can get, and I press my forehead against the coldwhite metal of the machine. I close my eyes. The vibration makes my skull feel like it's falling to pieces. Now that I cannot see the man, I can will him into the theoretical. I pretend that he's not there. I grind my teeth for 16 minutes until the cycle ends.

When I open my eyes the man is still there, closer than I remember, clenching his stroke fists, his pants around his ankles. I gather my wet clothes to my chest and stand for a moment. Another part of my original plan had been to exit through the back door and climb the stairs to my apartment, which sits directly above, then dry my clothes on the roof. I do not want the unwashed man to know where I live. I run out the front door and all of the underwear that I stole from my roommate scatters behind me like dead black rats.

~

I walk five blocks to the park. I drop most of my socks while I'm walking. I lay my clothes across the grass and lie myself next to them. I think about the ponygirl and I wonder where she is and I wonder if I can dress like something I'm not and charge people money to drag them around on a rickshaw. I wonder if the woman found her dead dog. I wonder if the man with the saxophone still has his saxophone, and if the man with the stroke fists has any medication. I wonder if the Down syndrome boy's parents love him and resent him in equal amounts. I wonder where my car is now. I wonder if my roommate knows that I stole her underwear. I think that the universe is a limitless box of possibilities opening into itself, and none of the possibilities seem good. I watch as a fog descends. I watch as the fog wets my wet clothes. I want to be able to say that I've done something with my life. I watch the sky and it's white as a feather. I don't want to be alone in the world. I rest my hand against my newly washed jeans and they are so very wet. I don't know what time it is or how long anything will take.

~

I don't know how long it has been raining when I wake up. My ability to sleep beneath unlikely circumstances has become a faculty of ghost-like sorts, and the only thing I am grateful for. It is the only thing I am grateful for, but I am only grateful for it when I am sleeping. When I am awake, I can only perceive my failure of absence.

In the dim of streetlight, I see a man heading toward me, brindled in fabric and plastic. I wonder where he's left his cart, and then I see what seems to be a glint of light against his hand. He walks with a brisk limp, like stray dog. I know that he sees me. I wonder if the glint is a knife. I don't move. I wonder if my roommates have wondered about me recently; about where I am; about if I am alone. I close my eyes again. I think muffled thoughts about my mother and my husband. In my thoughts, I cannot tell the difference between them.

I hear sounds like rustling and a smell that I know is another person beside me. I don't move. I hold my breath and I wait for something to happen.

There is breathing and raindrops. There is sighing. I wait and I wait and then I open my eyes because it's there's nothing else to do.

He looks straight through me. *Do you have a cigarette?* he asks and I tell him that I don't. *Do you have a lighter?* he asks and I pause a moment before sitting up and easing it out of my pocket. He clutches the lighter from my fingers and pulls a worn down butt from a crease of black plastic bag at his waist. He presses his lips and shields the flame against the wet. A twinge of wanting for something that isn't sleep. *Can*

I have some? I ask, even though the butt can't have more than two drags. He hands me the nub of cigarette and I suck until it's spent. He pulls another from his pocket and flicks the lighter again.

A GIN BLOSSUM STRUGGLES
| JAYINEE BASU

A gin blossom struggles to escape the ties binding him to the bed with a yellow FALL RISK sign taped to it. I ask him where he's going. To find my shoes, he said. If they untie me I can get my shoes and smoke a cigarette. They're not going to untie you, and if you don't calm down you're gonna undo your catheter and get pee all over yourself. Tell me about your shoes. They're under the bridge with Manny, he said. Who is Manny? Oh Manny is a good guy, those guys are all great, we go drinking all the time. Those were some good old times. Hey don't touch that, don't, don't, ok. You've undone the catheter. Good old times, we'd drink all night. He tears the FALL RISK sign. Hey, calm down. You are covered in pee, let's get you changed. His nurse comes over and gives me a look. It's better to stop him before he even tries to get up, he says. I wonder how that's possible. Look, don't you think you had better stop drinking? You're like a baby. The nurse says this kindly. The good old times. I support the gin blossom's red naked body as his nurse changes the sheets and helps him into a new gown. I am currently failing all my classes. I can't figure out how to stop myself before I try to get up.

SELECTIONS FROM *"THIS MUST BE THE PLACE"*
| *SEAN H DOYLE*

The Willow House, 3rd Ave and McDowell Road, Phoenix, June, 1994—

I come here after my shift at the record store and sit around at picnic tables outside, scribbling into notebooks while drinking shitty coffee and waiting for my girlfriend, Velvet, to get off work so we can go get high. The crowd here is varied: AA people alongside art people and punks alongside dirty Deadheads and downtown casualties. There are many open mic poetry events, usually outdoors at dusk. One night I decide to read. I go to the mic and drop weapons. I go to the mic and read about Kuwait City and southern Iraq. I go to the mic and read about prostitutes and hashish and drinking homemade wine made out of grape juice in the middle of the Indian Ocean. I go to the mic and curse over and over again. Nobody claps. Nobody moves. I am not asked to read again.

Warren 24th Apartments, 3024 N 24th Street, Phoenix, AZ Summer, 2002—

Living in this rent-by-the-week SRO is a nightmare but it beats sleeping in parks. Maggie contacted my grandmother and told her I had been on the streets for a long time and the two of them devised a plan to get a roof over my head. I am so fucked up from protecting myself and trying to feed myself that I end up with pneumonia. My friend Chris comes over to make sure I am eating and drinking enough water and he brings me an old TV and an old Playstation and a small sack of weed to try and bring my spirits up. We sit around smoking and playing NASCAR games and I start to feel more and more like a human being again. The other residents of the apartments are all destitute and shady, even more than I have become. They talk shit to me in the laundry room and when I am walking to my apartment and one of them flashes a gun at me one night and tells me he is going to kill my cracker ass.

One night a very drunk man smells weed coming from my apartment and tries to claw his way in through the window and when he pulls the screen off and finally has his arm inside of my room I stomp on his arm until I hear it break. He starts screaming and then the police and paramedics come and when they ask me why I stomped on his arm I tell them that he had been threatening me and had tried to break into my place twice before, which wasn't true, but felt true and felt safe. I do not feel bad about this lie.

Western Dental, 1820 N. 75th Ave, Phoenix, 2002—

I lied to the oral surgeon and told him I was allergic to morphine because I didn't want to get the urge to hunt it out after, so he ended up crushing and breaking and extracting my broken wisdom teeth without any pain medication. I told him the truth when I told him that lidocaine has no effect on me after years and years of abusing cocaine, so I felt almost everything he did to me. I felt like I deserved it all, like every shooting pain was something I had earned, like every bolt of lightning from my brain was a punishment due for past misdeeds. When he was finished I felt as if none of it was real and the endorphins surging through my body misled me into thinking I could ride the bus all the way home without incident. My mouth was bleeding so much that I had to keep spitting blood into an empty soda bottle and someone on the bus saw me and started freaking out and I had to explain to the driver what had happened and by the time I made it all the way home all I could do was smoke bowl after bowl of pot until I passed out.

Grand Street MTA Station, Chinatown, NYC, July 2005—

I had just piled a bunch of my grieving friends into cabs to get them to their hotels scattered across NYC after we'd spent the evening drowning ourselves in liquor after our friend Keith's wake. Everyone was shitfaced—my friend Allen even pulled a knife on the cabbie after I pushed him into the front seat with him, to show the cabbie he was from Texas—and I was no exception. I stumbled away from Motor City and made my way—somehow—to the subway station to catch the D back to Bensonhurst. I was so drunk I could not feel my teeth. I stood on the platform and started to sweat the liquor out of myself. I picked up a paper on the bench and it was all in Chinese and I got mad and then I started to take off my shoes. A woman was standing fifteen feet away, watching me, clucking her tongue. I took off my shirt, yelling about handjobs and death and how members of my family had just robbed me of half a million dollars. I took off my pants right as the train pulled in, waving them around so my wallet and money went flying everywhere. I tried to bend down and pick up my things as the doors to the train slid open and the rush of cool air engulfed me. I draped my pants over my shoulder and put my shoes on my hands and when I tried to grab my shirt I saw the woman who had been clucking her tongue had it in her hand and she and a man from inside of the train helped me get on.

I woke up on the platform at Coney Island.

I still could not feel my teeth.

SELECTIONS FROM *"THE ARSON PEOPLE"* | *KATIE JEAN SHINKLE*

STATE PENAL CODE (Excerpt)
Chapter XX
Arson & Burning

Section X00.110   Definitions

Sec. 110.

Any individual found engaging in the following
definitions as it pertains to and is defined by the
law could be found guilty of committing First,
Second, Third, Fourth, or Fifth Degree Arson.

Unless the context requires otherwise, the following terms have the following meanings:

(a) "Burn" means setting fire to, or doing any act
that results in, the starting of a fire, or aiding,
counseling, inducing, persuading, or procuring another to engage in such action.

997 Jug Factory Road

In the middle of the night this hot summer night Elsie Davis sneaks
out of her 2^(nd) story bedroom window, slides herself down the front of
the roof, drops herself onto the porch, and sprints through the woods
separating her grandmother's house and two streets over. Before she
enters the woods, she grabs a full, red, generic metal gas can and a box
of GoGreen! kitchen matches she hid underneath the formica trestle

attached to the front of the house. She called the elderly neighbor to the west earlier in the day when she knew her grandmother was out of gasoline to see if he had any. She always puffed her chest up extra when she had to make those phone calls, wanted to try to get in touch with a deeper voice inside, the man she knew she was. Even in summer she wears the heaviest clothing, today is a red and black plaid long-sleeved shirt with the sleeves rolled up and black leggings too small for her, which roll down. The neighbor called back but her grandmother answered, no gas for her. Later, Elsie Davis ate, sat on the corner of her bed until dark, and now she and the gasoline are leaving, around the half-fence her grandparents built to keep the raccoons out of the garbage. She is going as fast as she can through the woods. She is going to set Amber's house on fire. She is going to burn that bitch up.

112 Sprawl Road

Octavia is driving the car, Elsie Davis's grandmother's Cadillac, which they stole. They are keeping the headlights off but it is making it hard to see so every once in a while Octavia flashes the low beams. "We made a wrong turn. Let's go back," Octavia says and she puts it in reverse, mud and no traction. "We're going to have to rock it out," she says. Brewer and Elsie Davis get out and push the back end as Octavia, with the driver's side door open, guns the engine.

"One, two, three," Brewer grunts deeply, the car finally gives way, Elsie Davis falls knee first into the mud. Octavia barrels the car through the woods, leaving Brewer and Elsie Davis to walk the rest of the way to the house.

An extremely small, rustic cabin in the middle of nowhere is where Amber lives with her pedophile mother and mentally disabled older sister. Amber wears roller skates all the time and destroyed Elsie Davis's mini-trampoline once while jumping on it, popped a hole right through the top with one of the back wheels. Setting this particular house on fire feels hard for Elsie Davis. The place is so small: two windows, front and back, no stories, no front or back porch, a tiny concrete platform outside the sliding glass door (which doubled as the second window) and one vinyl braided beach chair, dirty, faded from the sun.

Elsie Davis knew the rumors about Amber's mother. Cut to the past: a young woman of only eighteen ran the only child care facility in town out of her house and got caught touching the older boys (eleven, twelve, thirteen respectively), how she got caught Elsie Davis did not know, and, years later, it all came to light. Amber's mother was shut down, and instead of fully relocating came out here with her two children. This cabin is all she has. This cabin with a sign outside every Halloween that says no child can ring for candy.

Amber's mother was currently screaming at her daughter, calling her a worthless fat piece of shit. When Elsie Davis hears this, it, for one brief moment, makes her feel sad for Amber, sorry for her.

8 Monte Vista, #9

Octavia and Brewer's mom is and was never around and so Octavia was home alone in an apartment a lot with her little brother, no more than a few years their junior, and Elsie Davis and Octavia and Brewer all hung out there all the time, today being no different than any other day.

Elsie Davis and Octavia and Brewer are together when they first hear about Gretchen. Girl Found Dead in Lake Michigan à Girl Found Dead in Lake Michigan Has Yet to Be Identified Due to the Violent Nature of the Assault à Girl Found Dead Has Been Identified as 17 Year Old Gretchen Steinberg. A week later: Girl Found Dead, 17 Year Old Gretchen Steinberg, Autopsy Reports Show Sexual Assault.

They are glued to the TV the entire day, cancelled their other plans with other people. They fielded phone calls but had no answers. They knew, however, who committed this crime. They knew before the boys were arrested, arraigned, got off. The media sympathized with them and their "blemish" in their decision-making; even this girl, Amber, who filmed it on her phone and did nothing to stop it, even when the footage shows Gretchen pleading with her, begging her to intervene, even this girl got sympathy for crying in court.

Gretchen Steinberg is raped by young men from their high school and then beaten to death and left in Lake Michigan and the young men walk. Here is where Elsie Davis and Octavia and Brewer decide to start paying visits.

CABLE TV

| M KITCHELL

I saw the strangest movie ever on cable one night. I mean, I guess it was a movie, I'm not sure; there were no credits or anything. I sat on my couch in the living room listening to the snow fall outside. I had left the radio on in another room. The muted television snow gave my eyes a pleasant zone of nothingness to focus on. It was three or four in the morning, and the blowing winter wind reminded me that it was far from dawn—whatever channel the television had been left on had long been off the air. I was exhausted, but my insomnia was inescapable. Desperate to sleep, I let my body get cold and stared at the television in front of me.

Thanks for tuning in to Nightdreams on KCUF, my name is Dave and I'll be your guide through this cold, sleepless night. A bit of a weather update before we get started here, it looks like before the sun rises the temp will drop a little below negative eight, so I'd recommend staying inside—which, let's face it, this late at night you oughta be inside anyway. Snow with heavy wind will continue all night long, so let's hope you can get used to those sounds. I'd suggest focusing on the repetition, let it lull you into a place of rest. Because rest is what we all really need. Once again, this is Dave here, and I'll be back after a few words from our sponsor.

With my windows vibrating from the wind, with the radio in the background playing anonymous soft jazz—my eyelids finally starting to sag toward a mental escape—until an image appeared on the screen.

I wasn't sure, at first. I reached my hand in front of my gaze toward the television. I considered touching the old glass plate on the tube TV. I wanted to measure this potentiality against haptic perception. Out of the static I began to recognize representational imagery in the dim flickering noise. Before long I could see the outline of a man, his body violently tossing itself in all directions in a desperate attempt at suppuration.

With the image becoming clearer, I could almost begin to make out details; a dark room with an asphalt floor, a small window spilling in the vaguest detail of light near the ceiling—the room had to be a basement, I mean, that's what it seemed like. While the man did not appear to be physically constrained in anyway, his insistent posturings carried the impotence of detention. As the man's face began to reach an acuity, my eyes were shocked with a blinding white— whiter than the snow falling outside, a pure light, a pure experiential excess. Squinting, I refused to tear my gaze away from the screen, wanting something, not knowing what. As my eyes adjusted to

What makes people all over America break down and cry like this?

Call 1-900-740-3500 and hear it for yourself.

Two dollars per minute. If you're under eighteen, ask your parents before you call.

1-900-740-3500

Now then, I want to make sure that all you listeners out there are feeling good tonight, I wanna make sure you're comfortable. I know that it can get cold and lonely on nights like tonight, and I know how not being able to sleep really hurts those feelings. If you wanna talk to

the light I could make out, once again, bodies, this time overexposed to the degree of an almost pure white—the white on whiteness of bodies climbing a hill.

A cut once again, this time revealing a more normalized image. A young boy standing outside a house, near the curb of the street. Analog artifacting digitized the ghost of his brief movements, indicating a sort of hyper-presence, the boy's silence filling the frame with minor desperation. The boy was crying.

I began to physically feel uncomfortable. Waves of what I could only describe as a difficult & abject nausea floated over my body. I realized it was the same feeling I had experienced when I read the letter my brother wrote me detailing the violent death of my best friend from childhood.

The boy stayed in the frame of the image far longer than the two earlier scenes. He walked around some, stared directly at the camera. The video used seemed somewhat cheap; primitive at least. The television signal was still weak and the ghosting intermittently returned. I moved closer to the screen.

Staring at the moire of the screen the video—the movie, film, whatever—cut to a close-up shot of the boy's face. The size of my television found the young

someone else who's up watching the blue moon through the wind at the same time as you, feel free to give me a call here at the station at any time. If you don't wanna talk though, sometimes the best way to make yourself comfortable when you're alone, when it's cold out, is to pour yourself a glass of wine and put on something that makes you feel sexy. Feeling sexy means you can take on the world, and when you close your eyes and just feel real good about what you look like, the cold just fades away, changing instead into a nice warmth. A nice warmth that will keep you feeling good.

We've got some good songs coming up tonight, some smooth jazz that will help you feel sexy, help you because that's why God put me on this green earth. I woke up one morning and a voice in my head told me, it said, "Dave, you're not doing anything with your life. You need to ditch this ego and focus on helping expression dwarfing that of my own. Within the relative distance of my face to the boy's I could feel infinity. It's like I understood what it meant to be blind. I reached out to touch the screen again, but this time I didn't stop myself. My hand reached the glass and I was shocked with the spark of static. On the screen the shot had cut back to a wide shot revealing more of the street. I could recognize the street as anywhere. It looked like summer and I tried to remember what it felt like to be warm. Time passed, though I have no idea of how long.

It was at this point that I realized it might be worth discovering what sound, if any, adjoined these images, so I turned away from the screen to try to find the remote. I had no luck, and by the time the television screen caught my eye again, there was something entirely new, something violating.

I felt the sound of a low rumble coming from somewhere. Maybe it was the radio, maybe the earth itself vibrating its dissatisfaction. A voice on the radio continued to talk with a calming lull, an ironic contrast to the images on the television.

The colors within the image flickered the blue and red necessities of the tubes. I wanted to smack the television to see if I could improve the quality, but was afraid

make other people feel good. Sometimes you might feel lonely, and that's ok, everybody feels lonely sometimes. But because you know this, Dave, it's time that you start helping other people out." And here I am today, guiding you through this cold night. Here's some music for you, dear listener, and this song right here, it's just for you.

[music]

Hope you enjoyed that lil' ditty right there, and just so you know there's more where that came from, soon as we get back from this commercial break.

She loved me, and she's gone. And I've entered, the secrets of her twilight eyes, whispers of my bedside, her arms, her mouth,

of interrupting the real. A scene from a talk show was playing out. The host sat at his desk in a suit while four women sat in arm chairs next to him. The man and three of the women were laughing, their bodies displaying hysterics. But the fourth woman, seated between the desk of the host and the other guests had an expression of terror. Something was wrong. She was screaming at these people, desperately trying to interrupt the fit of laughter. She stood up from her chair and flailed wildly in the direction of all the others, who paid her no attention. Tears began to shake from her eyes onto her manic face. She stared into the audience with the same intensity, screaming, screaming endlessly, while the laughter continued around her.

I found myself back on the couch, wrapped in a blanket, the cold from outside burrowing inside of me. I was overwhelmed with my own desperation now, I wanted someone, anyone, to acknowledge the manic woman.

But I knew that no one would.

So I watched. The woman's futility becoming an exercise in resistance. Tears streaked my own cheeks.

IN HEAVEN, EVERYTHING IS FINE.
IN HEAVEN, EVERYTHING IS FINE.
IN HEAVEN, EVERYTHING IS FINE.

Save me.

But how?

her amber hair—ah, the smell of it. She's deep in my blood, the only woman I'll ever love.

Love is child's play, once you've known obsession.

Calvin Klein's Obsession (ah the smell of it) at Maud & Taylor.

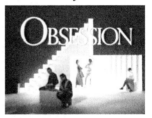

Welcome back to Nightdreams, Dave here, ready to give you the best sleepless night you've ever had. I hope everyone out there is feeling good right now, I hope everyone is feeling real smart on themselves, I hope you're relaxing, maybe drinking some wine or some bourbon, just feeling real good. I don't have much else to say right now, just wanted to remind you,

YOU'VE GOT YOUR GOOD THINGS,
AND I'VE GOT MINE.

The scene finally changed. My own body stopped shaking. We were back in the room that began the a-narrative sojourn of what I was watching. I saw the man again, clearer now. His body nude and strong. His body exhausted. It was then that I could see the water leaking onto the floor, slowly filling up the room. The man's body floated with the water as it rapidly began to rise. The water floating the man toward the ceiling, replacing air with wet.

Soon the entire room was full. A tank. The man floating inside, eyes shut, Harry Houdini in the dark. His eyes opened with a start, the scene changed to black. Fading, the black changed to noise.

The radio was now off the air. Time was gone. I could hear a drip from outside— the sun rising. But none of this made sense, for if the sun were rising both the radio and television station would be back on the air.

Shutting my eyes, I had no desire but that of warmth. I'm still flesh. The image was gone. Inside of my head I could hear a hum, a melody that I immediately assigned to what I had seen. And finally, I could sleep.

dear listener, of all of the night's potentialities. You can do whatever you want tonight, you can do whatever you need to do. And you can start by enjoying the sounds.

[music]

PRAMBLE

| DARBY LARSON

In Order to form the United States and establish the People of the United States and Justice, We establish a more perfect Justice. The People of the Union and Justice, We, to form, in Order to form a more perfect People of Justice. The United States of a more perfect Union, in Order to establish the People of We, form a more perfect Justice in Order to establish it. So, We form a more perfect establishing of Justice just as the People of Justice formed the United States before us. We the People of a more perfect Union establish the United States for a more perfect People of it. But in Order to insure the People of a more established Justice feel okay about it, the Union, in Order to insure the People of the Union, forms a more perfect People of the United States. This insures the People of the Union feel insured and a more perfect Union forms. The United States and the form of the Union, to establish Justice, forms a more perfect Union. Meanwhile, the People of the United States establish a more perfect People. The People of the Union, to insure the form of a more perfect Union, establish Justice in Order for the People of the Order to establish the Union. To insure the United States can establish the form of a domestic Justice, the establishment of a more perfect form of Justice insures the United States in Order to establish a more insured Union. So the United States, a more perfect Justice, and a more domestic Union are established. And the United States, to insure domestic form, establishes a more perfect form of itself and the Union of the United States forms a more perfect insurance. The Union, to form a more perfect United States, establishes, in Order to establish Justice, a more perfect and insured form of domestic Tranquility. The form of a more perfect and domestic Union establishes a more perfect Tranquility, a domestic Union, and an established Justice. As long as the established Tranquility feels insured, the form of the Union, in Order to insure a domestic

Union, reflects a more perfect Tranquility, and everybody's happy. So the domestically insured Union forms a more perfect Justice while the domestic Tranquility, in Order to form a more perfect Union, establishes a more insured Order. All of this is to insure a more perfect Tranquility, a more domestic Union, and a more insured Justice. This establishes Justice and insures domestic Tranquility. And that Tranquility, to provide for a more perfect Justice, forms a domestic Union and a more perfect means of establishing insurance. To establish Justice and to provide for a more perfect Union, insure a domestic form, and form a more perfect Tranquility to provide for. The Union and a more perfect form to provide for and insure domestic Tranquility, and establish a form of Justice more perfect than before. Tranquility, to provide for it, and a more perfect Union to establish and insure a domestic Justice everyone can agree on. The form of the Union, a more perfect one, and the Tranquility, the domestic one, insured for it. And the domestic Justice, insured, provides for the common Union and a more perfect Justice established. The common Tranquility across the Union is to insure the more perfect and common Tranquility is provided for. Establish Justice and provide for a domestic Tranquility and a more perfect Justice for the common Tranquility. The common Justice is established to provide for and insure the commonly established Tranquility. Or, rather, a more perfect Justice. Insure the Tranquility provides for the established Justice and the common, domestic Union provides for the domestic Justice. A more perfect and common, domestic insurance for the Union and a more perfect Tranquility. A more perfect defense provides for the established Union as well as the common Tranquility. The common defense provides for the Union which establishes Justice, insures a domestic common defense and provides for domestic Tranquility. Insuring domestic Tranquility is the common defense provided for and the established Justice insures it also. The common Union and the common defense are provided for to insure domestic Tranquility and to insure the Union establishes Justice. Insuring the Union establishes and insures the common defense is provided for by the Union itself along with the common Tranquility of Justice. The established Justice insures, provides for the common defense of, and promotes the domestic Tranquility for the commonly insured. Tranquility provides for Justice while Justice promotes and insures

Tranquility, and establishes the common defense of it. To provide for and promote the common establishment, the domestic and the insured, Tranquility promotes itself to Justice and the established defense of the insured. The common defense of the domestic Tranquility is to establish Justice and promote the common defense to provide for the insured establishment. Promote the common Tranquility before insuring Justice for the already provided for. That's common sense. Tranquility, Justice, provided for and promoted to establish the common defense. Insure domestic Tranquility, provide for the common general and the defense of it, plus Justice. Promote the general and provide for the domestic Tranquility of it. Justice, to provide for it and the common general, to insure the general is promoted, to defend the common Tranquility and the domestic commonality across it. The general and the common Justice, to insure a domestic providing for it, to provide for the common defense of it, to promote the general, and to insure Justice is the common defense of it. Justice and Tranquility, the common defense, the domestic general, all promoted. The common general, the domestic Welfare. To promote the Tranquility, the common defense, and the domestic Welfare. This insures the common defense insures the general Welfare and the domestic Tranquility of it. Insure the common Welfare and the defense of the provided for Tranquility provides for the general and the domestic and common insurance. The common Tranquility and the general defense and the common Welfare, the general. The common defense provides for domestic Welfare while the general Tranquility promotes the domestic defense for the general defense it provided Tranquility to. The common Welfare, meanwhile, insures the common defense, provides for the general Welfare and promotes domestic insurance. To secure the insurance provided for by the common defense securely defended by the general Welfare of Tranquility. To secure the domestic commonality is a must. The Welfare and the common Tranquility provided for by the promoted defense and the general domestic should provide for the promotion of the general Welfare securely. As long as the domestic Welfare and the domestic Tranquility are secured, the common defense and the common Tranquility will be domestically provided for and secured. Promoting the general Welfare is top priority. Providing for the common defense and securing the general Tranquility in defense of it. Not to mention the securing of the Blessings of it. To promote the Blessings of it. Securing and providing for the general Welfare, the common defense, Tranquility, and the Blessings. Defend the security of Tranquility by providing for the promotion of the common Blessings. Meanwhile, the general Welfare will have been provided for just as the common Tranquility, in defense of the Blessings, will have been promoted to secure the Blessings and provide for the common Welfare. The general Blessings and the common Blessings, the common defense and the Welfare of it. Tranquility, providing for the common defense, secures the Blessings and promotes the general defense. Provide for the common defense, the general Welfare of Liberty, securely, the common Welfare and the security of the general Blessings of Liberty. The Welfare and the common Liberty secures the Blessings of the defense of a general attitude. Basically, promoting the Blessings and securing Liberty are part of the common defense provided for by the Blessings, in hopes that the defense of the common and general Welfares agree with each other. Lest providing for the Blessings of Liberty becomes the securing of the general Welfare and the general Welfare sees fit to provide for the common defense of it. To ourselves, the Blessings appear common, so the promotion of the general Welfare is secured. The Blessings of Liberty to ourselves is secure. The common defense is secure, and the Blessings are promoted to ourselves and the general security of our Welfare. The common Blessings to ourselves feel secure and common, the defense of the Welfare to ourselves feels promotable to ourselves. Ourselves are the common defense promoted by the general Welfare, secured by the Blessings of a common Liberty to ourselves. The common defense, the general Welfare, the promoted Blessings, ourselves, of Liberty. The Blessings of ourselves feel common. To secure Liberty, the general Posterity of the Blessings, and the Welfare of it, along with the general defense of our Posterity of Welfare, a more general promotion is secured. So Liberty, a more defensive Welfare, and the Blessings of Liberty. Liberty, to secure the Blessings of our Posterity, in general, a defense of our Posterity from itself and the promotion of Liberty promote a more defensive security. The promotion to ourselves and our Posterity are a defensive Liberty, a promoted general Welfare, and ourselves to secure and keep secured our Posterity of the Blessings of Liberty. The general Welfare promoted, our Posterity secured by the Blessings. Do ordain and secure the Blessings of Liberty, ourselves for the Posterity and the general Liberty, plus Welfare. Promote the general and ourselves for the Blessings and the Liberty of it. Welfare, to ourselves and the general Posterity, to secure the general Welfare, to promote the Posterity of Liberty and the Blessings of Posterity. The general Welfare and the Posterity of Welfare, to secure the Blessings and the ordaining of it to ourselves and for Posterity. Welfare and Liberty, the Posterity promotion, the general Blessings, all promoted. The Liberty of Posterity, do ordain and secure the Blessings of Welfare. To secure the Liberty of our Posterity, do ordain and establish the Welfare for the general Blessings to ourselves and our security. The Blessings to ourselves establish the ordaining of the Welfare and its generalities. Of Liberty, to ourselves, our Posterity, Blessings secured, do ordain the Welfare to ourselves. Secure the Blessings. Our Posterity and the Liberty established by the Posterity of our general Welfare. Our Posterity ordains and does. Ourselves and our secured Blessings establish the general Welfare of our Posterity. Secure the Liberty before the Posterity establishes the Blessings to ourselves. Do ordain and establish the Blessings to ourselves and our Posterity of Liberty. And here we have the Blessings of this Constitution, to ourselves, and the securing of Liberty in order to do the ordaining and establish it. Although the Welfare is securely established of Liberty, ourselves and our Posterity do ordain the securing of this Constitution of Liberty and Welfare. Our Posterity, established by this Constitution, constitutes the Blessings that established it to ourselves and our Posterity. Do ordain and establish this Constitution for the established Blessings of Constitutions everywhere. Of Liberty, securely, establish ourselves and the secured Welfare of Liberty. Establish our Posterity and this Constitution securely. To ourselves, this Constitution of Posterity establishes Blessings and Welfare. Establishing this Constitution to ourselves secures the United States of America from ordaining the doing of the securing of Blessings to ourselves and our Posterity. The Constitution of the Blessings of Liberty secures this Constitution for the United States of America ordainly. Our Posterity, our Liberty, to ourselves, securely, this Constitution of Liberty, do ordains and establishes Liberty and Posterity to ourselves, to the Blessings, to a new Constitution, established for the

United States of America. Establish the United States of America and secure its Blessings, its Constitution, and its Posterity. Do ordain and establish the Blessings of the United States of America.

A SELECTION FROM *"ANTIGOLF"*
| *JOHN COLASACCO*

As an experiment the family brought thing after thing into the house. As each thing occupied a certain amount of space, eventually the house grew completely full.

The family stood outside the full house and attempted to draw conclusions.

"At least now we know how much can go in," said the dad.

That was true; I myself took the measurements.

"At least now we can focus on what should go in and what shouldn't," said the mom.

I hadn't thought of this, but it seemed correct.

"We can take the things out now?" said the sister.

"We could but we won't," said the dad.

\>\>

So the house remained full of things in boxes, with the biggest boxes layering the floors up to the sink the medium boxes filling to the ceiling the small boxes filling in irregularities between the others and in the crevices and finally very tiny boxes stuffed up the faucets.

In the big boxes were clothes, trophies, bears, used and unused stationery, also broken-down desks, organizers, camping sets, canned food, boxed dry cereal, bread, eggs, fresh fish, vegetables, crackers, rum, wine, salve, soap, dishes, rags, laundry detergent, astringent, a guitar, a cello, a whole frozen pig, Christmas things, a training toilet, a paper shredder, paper plates, a fishing rod, soccer shoes, a soccer ball, and two size large orange traffic cones.

In the medium-sized boxes were thousands of other large orange cones. Nothing else.

I took an extra look at these, and packed them myself, quite densely.

After that, none of the boxes contained anything but crumpled paper to prop them up, like suitcases for sale . . .

>>

For the sake of the experiment, the boxes were also said to contain something "intangible."

But who could prove it?

>>

The only obstacle in constructing the experiment was that the house couldn't be filled completely; if you were the one inside the house, filling it with the last few boxes, the very space you took up would keep the house from being totally full.

The family solved this by cutting the house in half and filling the two halves separately, then putting them roughly back where they had been before.

So the house teetered a bit as they studied it.

And it had a seam down the middle, with small boxes leaking out.

>>

The family continued to study the house as a family.

Then the dad went over and tried to scoop some of the leaked boxes back in.

He kept trying to get one tiny box to stay in the seam, but it kept falling.

I went over to help him.

When I got there he motioned me closer, like he had a secret to tell me.

"Don't say anything to your mother or your sister, but this house is no good. We can't live in it anymore."

"I thought about that when we started," I said.

"I did, too," he said.

"Did you?" I asked.

"Yeah–I did–back when I was changing your fucking diaper!"

>>

I stopped helping him and went back to tell others what I knew.

They were both sitting in the grass now, being quiet.

My sister asked, "Are we taking the stuff out now?"

"I think so. . . Yes," I said.

I wasn't sure myself why I said that to her.

"Then why does he keep trying to fill it back up?" asked my mom.

"I think he's almost done," I said.

>>

The old man was up on a ladder now, stuffing the last few leaked-out boxes into the roof seam.

I put my own ladder against the house and climbed up.

"Did you tell them?" he asked me.

"No... But I might."

He stuffed the last few boxes in the seam.

"Well, hey, don't do me any favors..."

He pushed past me and climbed down.

I didn't know what to do.

>>

I held my breath and jumped into the seam on the roof, causing the boxes I displaced to cascade off onto the lawn.

I heard the old man cursing at me.

I wormed my way down through the top layer of boxes.

The weight of all of them crushed in on me as I half swam, half sank into crevices.

I burrowed down through the groaning attic stairs; I burrowed down through the bottlenecked landing to the second floor, where I found my way to the medium-sized boxes, and started unpacking the cones.

>>

The first medium box was the hardest; once it unsealed I was able to use the cones inside to help me pry open more working space for myself.

I wedged the cone tips between the boxes that surrounded me and created a small round cockpit in the heart of the house.

I switched on a penlight and held it in my teeth.

From there I had room to get down to the large boxes.

I opened these one at a time, until I found the food.

>>

A few hours later I gasped as several of the cones forming the ceiling of the cockpit caved in.

Then my sister crashed through, also gasping for breath.

She helped me fix the ceiling and helped me wedge more cones in to give us more space.

Eventually we extended the cockpit chamber all the way to the window.

Real light came in.

We opened the window and peered down.

There were our parents, fighting (in their way.)

We watched our dad frantically attempt to stuff an enormous quantity of displaced boxes back into the house, while our mom sat there, wounded, on the grass.

"This was stupid," I told her. "We'll be crushed.

"And look at poor Mom!"

My sister put down her cracker.

"Let's knock it down, then." she said.

>>

I agreed.

I didn't really think we had enough leverage between us, but I started to figure in my head just how much force it would take for us to push the sides of the house apart, given what I knew about the house's center of gravity, the properties of the soil, weight distribution . . .

But just then we overheard our parents fighting again down on the lawn.

We crowded close to the window and listened in.

From what we could tell it sounded like they were already one step ahead of us.

Instead of filling the house, they would take things out—even the two of us.

Our father was in the process of convincing our mother tit would be best to take all the walls down, and all the stairs out, and all the air out.

Even the intangible things. . .

A SELECTION FROM "LAST MASS"
| JAMIE IREDELL

I am a Catholic. I was baptized Catholic as a baby, and Mom raised me as such. Dad converted, and became Catholic. My brother and sister are Catholics. Grandma and Grandpa were Catholics. My uncles are Catholic. My uncles' wives are Catholic. My cousins are Catholics. My aunt's husband's family is Catholic. His sisters' names are Faith, Hope, and Charity. I used to feel guilty after I masturbated. I am Catholic.

In the first Station of the Cross, Jesus—expressionless, haloed, his shoulders and wrists rope-bound—stands beside a scroll-wielding Pilot. No filth dirties the building. No age smudges the architecture. No raw sewage strews a gutter. Everything then was new, a world so new even the distant mountains sit wrinkleless. Roman soldiers jeer in the background. Said background is lavish: columns, drapes, blue sky, solitary cloud.

The highway's shoulders splashed green with Indian grass butting up against the asphalt and backed by white pines, red oaks, sycamores, maples, all rolling into the hills that gradually ascended into Georgia's Appalachian foothills and into the Appalachians themselves. The merest hint of autumn—splashes of yellow islands—hung out there in glimpses that my speed and gaps in the tree line along the highway afforded me of the forested countryside.

The priests baptized Miquel Josep Serra a Catholic, born 1713 in Petra, Mallorca. Twenty years before this birth, the Spanish Inquisition held *autos de fé* in Palma, Mallorca's capital, and Jews were burned at the stake. Four more *conversos* were burned in 1720, when Miquel was seven. For his Holy Orders, Miquel Josep adopted the name of one among Saint Francis's favorites, and he became Father Fray Junípero

Serra, of the Order of Friars Minor. Later he became a *comisario* of the Holy Office of the Inquisition.

I went to the mountains of north Georgia, to a tiny cabin, so that I might write about how I am from California, and that Blessed Father Fray Junípero Serra was among the first people of European descent to set permanent feet in California. Like it was for the venerable Father's Native converts years ago, for me the Catholic Church, and my California past, and the me who I was when I went into these mountains—all of it—seemed an insurmountable bear.

Grizzly Man, Timothy Treadwell, got ate up by the bears he loved, his abdomen ripped open, the surrounding skin paled, his staring eyes vacant as the scream still etched across his face. Bowels and ribcage.

In photos I do tummy time on imitation sheepskin rugs, red-capped, two-toothed smile. I ramble my parents' backyard lawns, watering (or attempting to) the *Agapanthus*, poured into a denim short panted jumper, my hair brown and naturally blond highlighted, straight as a mop atop my head. Now the hair's curly and brown. I look very happy, happy little Catholic boy spilling his ice cream down a tiny dress shirt. Now I am dirty.

History knows little about Blessed Father Fray Junípero Serra's early years. His parents were farmers who kept up a hovel in Petra. The ground floor contained the future Apostle of California's bedroom and the animals' stable. Miquel Josep was sickly and small, growing to a mere five feet, two inches in adulthood—shorter than my wife. As eighteenth century things went, expectedly, Miquel Josep's siblings all died. The strongest presence in Mallorca was the Church. Franciscans founded the Lullian University in Palma, to which Miquel Josep applied. For having lived in Enlightenment Europe, Blessed Father Fray Junípero Serra's life and worldview was definitively medieval.

Blessed Father Fray Junípero Serra took his Doctor of Philosophy at the Lullian University, and there met two lifelong friends: Fathers Fray Francisco Palou and Juan Crespí, students. Together the three missioned to Nueva España then to Baja California, and finally to Alta California. They would found nine missions in what is today the American State of California. At Blessed Father Fray Junípero Serra's deathbed Father Fray Francisco Palou administered extreme unction and last rites. Father Fray Junípero Serra would be buried beside the already-deceased Father Fray Juan Crespí, where together they still lie, beneath the bronze sarcophagus and the stone floor of La Basilica de San Carlos de Borromeo, in Carmel, California, the city in which I was born.

In high school I took girls to Mission San Carlos. The courtyard draped with bougainvillea and African daisies, the fountains gurgling in tune with the swallows' songs. I knew a stone bench recessed in a bower of roses. There's nothing like Catholicism for drawing out teenagers' urges.

Father Fray Junípero Serra founded La Misión de San Diego de Alcalá, around which grew the City of San Diego; and La Misión de San Carlos de Borromeo—Monterey; and La Misión de San Francisco de Asís—the City of San Francisco. He helped to found El Pueblo de Nuestra Señora de Los Angeles del Rio Porciuncula: original name of the City of Los Angeles. His Misión de San Luis Obispo de Tolosa became the City of San Luis Obispo. And La Misión de Santa Clara, around which grew the City of Santa Clara, was also founded by the venerable Father, and lies in today's Silicon Valley, where are found all the implements we've created that have brought us closer to thinking of ourselves as gods.

First of the Seven Sacraments: Baptism. For Catholics, Confirmation is baptism *numero dos*. At what the Catholic Church has deemed the *age of reason*, after instruction in the Holy Faith, a bishop confirms the confirmand. Usually, only a bishop performs this Sacrament, except in some cases, where the power's granted to priests. Fray Junípero Serra, in a Pontifical Brief, obtained a ten-year patent to confirm the neophytes of Alta California.

Confessor Junípero Serra was prelate to Fathers Juan Crespí and Francisco Palou. Catholic priests have as many titles as the universe galaxies.

Junípero Serra should additionally be titled Blessed, due to his 20th century beatification. Technically, Blessed Father Fray Junípero Serra would need one more miracle confirmed by the Roman Curia before canonization to sainthood; however, His Holiness, Pope Francis has announced his intention to canonize the blessed father. Blessed to many faithful. Blessed are the Native Californians who protest this anticipated canonization.

I tried to calm myself from my apprehension over this trip into the Georgia mountains by listening to the mixed CD my wife had made for me before she was my wife, back when our love was so new even the case that housed this CD hadn't cracked. Her mix hit every emotion, as all mix CDs ought to, specific as they are for their intended audience, and anything but sentimental for an outsider. Yes, this CD included Journey.

I attended Catechism at Our Lady of Refuge, in Castroville, California, my home parish, part of the Diocese of Monterey, a diocese founded by the Blessed Father Fray Junípero Serra. In Catechism we colored in Catholic coloring books, and made for our parents construction paper cards that depicted Mary and Joseph, and the appearance of the Archangel Gabriel before Mary upon the Annunciation. We drew symbols of the Holy Trinity—dove, crucifix, P exed with an X (the chi-rho), the triquetra—and celebrated the sanctity of mother and fatherhood. This instruction prepared me for the second of the Seven Sacraments: Holy Communion.

At my First Communion I wore a tiny shirt and tie, like all the other boys. The girls wore elaborate and frilly white gowns. All of us eight-year-olds marrying the Lord.

At the Lullian University Father Serra zealously sought to be a missionary to what he and other Europeans of the time called *the heathen* of New Spain.

On Father Serra's zeal: our English word comes to us from the Greek ζῆλος: transliterated: *zelos*: used in ecclesiastical Latin to describe one with great enthusiasm and energy for God. Today, a derivation—*zealot*—is still used to describe the faithful, but can carry also a negative connotation, as in *Among the zealots of Islam are suicide bombers*, or, *Christian zealots preach that "God hates fags."* In the case of Father Serra, *monomaniacal* is perhaps a more appropriate modern adjective to combine with zeal: so great was Father Serra's monomaniacal zeal for bringing the Gospel to the Natives of North America, that he was willing—in fact hoping—to die in the process.

I spent every Sunday morning in mass at Our Lady of Refuge. Mom roused me from bed, had me dressed in Sunday clothes, and we rushed off in our attempt to make it on time, the station wagon's tires squealing as she floored us out of our housing development onto Highway 156 heading towards Castroville.

In George Lucas's 1977 film *Star Wars* the ghostly voice of the deceased character Obi-Wan Kenobi (indeed, he vanished, leaving nothing but a monastic-looking robe) encourages his former student Luke Skywalker to *Use the Force*. Immediately following this, in a jump cut, the film's antagonist, Darth Vader, preparing to laser the young starfighter into vapors floating in the Death Star's gravitational pull, exclaims, *The Force is strong in this one*. It appears that Darth Vader regularly talks to himself.

Conversos are Jews forced to Catholicism by the Holy Office of the Inquisition. Though the medieval Church suspected all Jews, even those who might have sincerely converted.

The curious eyes of priests spying a converso's home, noting that no smoke emitted skyward come Sabbaths. The priests condemned conversos as heretics, and forced them into confessions. A parade through the cobbled Palma streets from the Jewish Quarter to the plaza, your fellow Mallorcans tossing curses and molded tomatoes, your arms bound, grape-pelted. The platform seating the bishop and priests, the *alcalde*, and other notables of your city in attendance, four thousand eyes. The post upon which you're bound. The fires lick your toes, your heels, your shins. The pain searing, and your screams unmuffled by the silent rapturous crowd. Finally the pain numbed, and your vision of the blue sky, the smoke, scent of roasting human flesh—yours—your vision darkening, then black. The last sound is the hiss of your own fat flaring in the flames.

AVENUE C

| BRANDON HOBSON

—Drugging him seems dumb. So does stalking him. I'm not a stalker. You'd think he'd mention the films to someone.

—That scene in *City Lights* at the end. Chaplin's face. The blind girl. One of the saddest movies I've ever seen. Fucking thing kills me every time. What is it about that last scene? What is it about Chaplin's tramp that makes him so sad?

—That scene in *The Kid* when they're reunited.

—Are we even sure he has them? I'm still up in the air about it, which is why we have to be careful.

—What I like about this group is the trust. Go anywhere and look around. What do you see? People standing around, concerned only with themselves.

—I miss that fucking dog. Sorry, guys.

—Drugging him and going through all his shit is the only way. I don't see any other way ending well.

—Senator Bowery is a large man. My wife thinks he looks like Hitchcock. I see the resemblance. If he has the films, I think we would've heard about it by now. It makes much more sense for Chaplin to have them.

—Swaggert wrote Chaplin the letter and hasn't heard back. No phone call, text, email. Nothing. I knew it would be ignored.

—Armadillos carry leprosy, which is something most people don't think about. Who goes around touching a carcass? But they're splattered all over the road. Go down any highway or country road. They're all over the fucking place.

—I'm about three shock treatments from losing it.

—We've got to get his kid out of there. We shouldn't involve the kid. You assholes start involving kids and I'll question your goddamn morals.

—I'm filming something with Bolivian cut coke. Top secret. Just you wait.

—Walking the streets at night, the ghosts of Lillian Gish, Louise Brooks, and Greta Garbo. They're being seen in town more. They escaped the Nugget Hotel.

—I'll be serious a moment. There was a time when I did a hit of acid alone on my back porch. I was out of it, sitting there watching two birds hop in the grass. One of the birds, I remember, had a worm or something in its beak and it gave the worm to the other bird. I thought that was amazing. I've never seen anything like it. Maybe it sounds dumb, but I realized in that moment life's secret, which is to be a giver. We can sit around here all night pissing up each other's tree. We can argue, be pissed off, whatever. But I wanted to take those two birds into my house and keep them forever. It was as real a spectacle as anything I've ever seen.

—Someone left their cock ring here last night.

—He's right, goddammit. Mishityu?

—Anyway, that clip of the Academy Awards, when Little Feather refused the Oscar on behalf of Brando. How he managed to get away with it. It would never work now. You can't do anything that good. You can't beat that.

—Pepi Lederer. Mary Pickford.

—Can't we come out and ask the son of a bitch? I don't get it. Last time I checked people were honest about who they are.

—I mean the Oriental girl who gives the foot job.

—What I want to know is how to get past all those fucking armadillos around Chaplin's building. It's all Jasper's fault, the sick fucker.

—I read something in one of those rock magazines about Caspar Fixx starting a cult. Does he still do heroin? I'm telling you, Senator Bowery knows everything about him.

—Look, Eddie. I trust Swaggert like an uncle. I'd trust Dominick, Stan, Lou with my kid. With my life. These guys have changed my life. What else is there to say? We're like a family.

—It's about my loneliness.

—Loneliness and manipulation.

—We have to keep after him, Arnold. It's dangerous but we have to do it.

—Stop calling me Arnold. All I'm saying is it's a huge risk to keep after it this intensely. There are still too many unanswered questions.

—Chaplin in his older age. He was rarely recognized. He could be sitting in a restaurant, white-haired, old, wearing a suit and nobody would come up to him. Do you ever wonder if he was lonely despite all the children?

—The sexploitation films of the sixties. There's the one with Yoko Ono where she gets attacked. There's the one with the woman who's tied and gagged and confronted sexually by a group of motorcycle guys. The guys look really normal though, even for the sixties.

—Do it and see what happens, Mishityu.

—...the snuff films...

—...the noises, the smells. The weird stuff. Something about actual death caught on film, the fascination with fire, blood...

—something about suicidal thoughts and the way you know you're going to die on film...

—The hallucinations, the sounds, the noises. The smells. All the paranoia.

—They found the poor thing in an alley. It wasn't moving.

—The Oriental girl in the Blackwelder District. In the back room. Have you met her?

—Smooth and hairless.

—Helen Jerome Eddy. Pauline Frederick.

—Name Peter Sellers's best movie.

—They never finished doing it. They kept dicking around before anyone ever fucking finished. How are we supposed to get anything done?

—I'm not kidding, Arnold. His name was Mick. I miss him.

—Charlie Chaplin's speech at the end of *The Great Dictator*.

—I fell in love with many people, but the main one was a writer who never became famous. Her name was Catherine and I called her Cat. I read all her stories, even the ones she didn't give me. I especially loved the ones about me. The boys she named in her stories were all based on me. But I always understood the complexities surrounding her situation. Later she married and had children. She was afraid to move out of her comfort level.

—I dreamed of walking the streets of Paris with her. In one of the dreams someone was playing a guitar in front of a small shop. Possibly in real life I wished she was French. I do not remember if I told her so.

—The story goes, as a child I spoke French in my sleep. I was able to fly around the room in our big house singing songs while my brothers and sisters were asleep upstairs. My grandmother says the feathers we found outside were mine.

—Some days I wanted to read there, by the window, but my brothers and sisters were loud. I wanted to go sit somewhere quiet. I went to the library. I always sat at the same table upstairs. There was an erotic Japanese painting called 'Dream of the Fisherman's Wife' that showed an octopus sexually devouring a woman's body. Mostly I sat there just to look at that painting.

—I still get aroused very easily.

—Oof.

—You ever read the obituaries in the *Observer*? People are dying strange deaths. Last week someone fell seven stories from the roof of a building downtown. Two teenage lovers put on their seat belts and drove a Toyota into the lake and drowned. Bad things keep happening.

—He's right. In a field east of Route three, a farmer named George Hinton shot himself in the head with a thirty-eight special revolver a week after his wife of forty years died of a heart attack. I could see Hinton's house in the country outlined in a strange armature of blue morning light. The darkened, endless land around it holding the ghosts of the men who worked sixteen hour days in those fields, farm workers who had dropped out of school at age fourteen to work with their fathers and grandfathers and came home hurting every night.

—That sure is pretty, what you said.

—It's about the fantasy, not real life. It's the fantasy.

—I'm pushing fifty, Arnold. Previously I was a prince from the Greek and Slavic monastic circles. I had a girlfriend once who told me I would likely die before I was forty. She wanted to mother me. She wasn't really my girlfriend.

—Everybody needs to be a part of something. I went to a sexual addiction conference. Everyone should go.

—Despite the loneliness I have to learn to trust everyone here. We all do.

A SELECTION FROM "PLAYDATE"
| MARK KATZMAN

I have the house all to myself now.

Mother and Father are here but they're not talking.

This will take all night. In the morning I shall finish the job. Perhaps after a game of pool. Yes, that's how it will be. They'll find me sprawled across the red felt with my little ass in the air.

Good. Settled. We can move on.

You look peaceful, Mother. I'm going to touch you up a bit.

There.

I want you to look your best. Father too.

Family occasions are so rare.

I came home on a Tuesday. It was raining. There was a buzzing in my ears. I think it was a Tuesday. I think it was home.

The car pulled into the driveway and I saw a large scorpion on the roof.

I closed my eyes and took several deep breaths.

The driver opened the door and helped me out.

His clothes were identical to the ones worn by all the male attendants at the clinic: black beret, turquoise shirt, gold sports-jacket, maroon pants, white patent-leather shoes.

His name was Jones. That's what his tag said. He didn't speak a word during our time together. Our days. Our weeks.

I did not speak, either, having taken a vow of silence long ago.

The front door opened.

A woman stood in the doorway with bright blue hair shaped into a bee-hive.

Mother?

"Welcome home, M.," she said.

Jones drove off without saying goodbye.

We walked down a long hallway.

I was transfixed by her hair.

She was wearing a white uniform with the initial K embossed in black on the side of each shoulder.

Her short dress. White spiked heels.

I liked her white stockings and garter-belt very much.

In my room. At long last. The buzzing in my ears was gone.

I undressed and put on the black silk pajamas.

The woman knocked twice and came in. She was wearing a low-cut white jump suit. The K in yellow on each shoulder.

She held a silver tray.

"Your Grandmother is in the room just off the kitchen," she said. "Yesterday she told me the flowers on the kitchen table were on fire. Before that it was children singing inside the closet. Enjoy your lunch and don't forget to take your pills."

Lunch was a raisin-bread and cream cheese sandwich with orange juice.

There were three pills. Two were green, oval-shaped, and very small. The third was a large capsule filled with tiny pink and green pellets.

I took them after finishing lunch.

In a few minutes my body was numb.

I closed my eyes and saw a woman embedded in a block of ice. She had long black hair and pale skin and she was very beautiful.

Then she decomposed.

There was a vivid array of lights before I lost consciousness.

Night. I heard the scorpion on the roof. After a minute or two it moved away. All was silent again.

The hallway was pitch black. I felt along the wall until I reached the kitchen. I stood there while my eyes adjusted to the dark.

I found a flashlight in a drawer by the sink.

Down the hallway. Open the front door.

The scorpion was facing me on the driveway. A menacing thing several feet long.

I shone the light into its eyes. It began clicking its pincers furiously.

I shut the door and returned to my room.

From my window I noticed a light on next door. A woman with blonde hair was sitting at a desk, writing.

A SELECTION FROM "EVERYONE GETS EATEN"
| BEN BROOKS

Do not approach dinosaurs.

Do not shout disparaging remarks at dinosaurs.

Do not, even in the privacy of your own homes, make jokes about dinosaurs.

Do not, even in your dreams, attempt to wrestle dinosaurs.

Do not attempt to placate dinosaurs with offerings of milk or unwanted siblings.

Do not draw dinosaurs.

Do not curl up and cry late at night, after three cartons of milk, imagining dinosaurs pulling you apart like wet paper.

Do not pull each other apart like wet paper over arguments concerning the nature of dinosaurs.

Do not concern yourself with the nature of dinosaurs.

Do not ask the people above the clouds for help with dinosaurs.

Do not blink in the presence of dinosaurs.

Just don't.

Okay?

*

In The Doll Hospital, Casper watched Dr Sixteen press his stethoscope against the chest of a plastic baby. The doctor closed his eyes and shook his head. Casper sipped milk. He was sitting on an empty bed, swinging his heels into the metal frame.

'Stop it,' Sixteen said.

'Sorry,' Casper said, not stopping. 'Are you going to tell me what to do?'

'No. I'm not going to tell you what to do. You should have asked what to do before you did what you did.'

Casper squinted as though it would help him understand. Sixteen was only four and a quarter but he spoke like someone double that. They had been close for three years. Casper was often falling into holes and Sixteen was often pulling him out of them. Sometimes, never purposely, Casper would push his friend into holes and find himself totally unable to help him climb out. That always made his stomach sink.

The doctor moved along to the next bed, again pressing his stethoscope to pretend pink skin and listening intently. Casper raised his voice. 'They want to give me a new house.'

'I'm trying to work.'

'In The Meatball District.'

'Are you going to take it?'

'No.'

'Good.'

'Why good?'

'Because when this ends how it will inevitably end, they'll be less upset if you haven't accepted whatever dumb gifts they're offering.'

Casper tipped a long stream of milk down his throat, placed the carton on the bedside table, and lay down. 'It might not end like that.'

'If it doesn't end like that, we can swap houses.'

'You'll live in The Cardboard Hill?'

'If I'm wrong.'

Casper opened his mouth to reply, stopping himself as a junior nurse sidled up to Sixteen and presented him with a clipboard. On the clipboard was a red heart drawn above a flat black line. She pointed at a cot in one corner of the room. The doctor nodded and passed back the clipboard.

'What did it say?'

'Same as it always says.'

A door swung shut as the junior nurse disappeared. Casper rolled onto his front. 'Have you told Diana?'

Diana was Sixteen's wife. She worked as a fireman in The Origami Quarter and still believed in the voices above the clouds. She disliked her husband's only friend and encouraged their disentanglement. It wasn't that Casper seemed particularly bad, just that he never expressed concern or care for anything. She wanted him to care about something, anything, even if it was only fish spotting or sketching charcoal doodles of his own feet.

'Absolutely not. If she knew, I wouldn't get to play with you at all.'

'You never play with me at all anyway.' He drained the last of his milk. 'Come down to the bar.'

'I can't. I have a job.'

'I'm trying to get a job. I'm making a job for myself.'

'You're not trying to get a job. You're trying to get a girl.'

Casper stared at the ceiling, picturing Tatiana and then George. His future with Tatiana was resting on the shoulders of George. Tiny, shaky George, who didn't know left from right and could only count up to fourteen. The only person he knew who would agree to the plan. The only person capable of spectacularly ruining the plan.

'Can I ask something?' The doctor said, hanging the stethoscope from his neck and turning to face his one friend.

'Yes.'

'Why did you suddenly decided to do this? You never said about doing this before. It's been a long time since Tatiana didn't want to sit next to you.'

One of Casper's shoes nudged the either. His gaze locked onto them. 'She's connected to Kevin now. I watched by the cathedral, they were in each other's noses.'

*

The sky slid from pink to orange as one set of presenters left the radio tower and a new set arrived. Avery and Pele liked to count the steps out loud and in unison as they ascended them. There were one hundred and eighty-four. Another thing they liked to do was knock each other down.

Pele jabbed his elbow into the back of Avery's knee. Avery collapsed. He stood up. He was wearing shorts. A drawbridge of skin hung open from his knee.

'What did you do that for?'

'What do you mean? We always kick each other.'

Pele had been eating a bacon double cheeseburger. Avery had been pulling splinters from the sides of his fingernails with his teeth.

'We don't kick each other anymore. There are dinosaurs now. It's not appropriate.'

Pele took a bite the size of a lemon, releasing a trickle of brown grease down his chin. He replied with a full mouth. 'There aren't dinosaurs.'

Avery took a step back. 'Yes there are. And the night is coming.'

'People always say 'the night is coming.' What does that even mean? It's stupid. I don't see any night.'

'That's the point, you don't see it until it's here. Everything turns so slowly grey that you don't notice it until it's not grey anymore.'

'That won't happen.'

'Yes, it will.'

With a karate chop, Avery knocked the burger from his co-host's hands.

'That was my burger.'

'Don't brag.'

'What?'

'We're late.'

In silence, they continued climbing until they reached The Globe. The Globe was a giant glass ball containing the radio studio and a members-only café patronized by business owners and councilmen. At two hundred feet, it was the tallest building in Billion, as well as the most expensive and most frequently insulted (the bald ghost, the blob, the worst stupidest thing ever made by anyone ever, and so on).

The producer nodded to them as they fell into monogrammed swivel chairs and donned oversized headphones. Neither presenter returned the nod. Skull-sized mugs of Darjeeling appeared before them. They waited for the crossover track to play out then began to talk.

'You're listening to Nine FM with Pele Marti—'

'And Avery Vitafit. The sky is currently mint green, there are fourteen clouds, and it's shorts weather.'

'No, it isn't.'

'Yes, it is.'

'You're wearing shorts and you have goosebumps.'

'Because you pushed me onto marble steps, you table.'

'That isn't how you get goosebumps.'

'It is, if you have sensitive—'

The producer took them off air, replacing their voices with a short pre-recorded documentary about active volcanoes in Japan. He asked what was going on. Before they answered, he told them that he didn't care what was going on. He told them to shove whatever was going on up themselves and pull it back out of their ear holes. He asked if they wanted to keep their boxy villas and their pedal cars. They told him they did. They agreed to surrender. They averted each other's eyes and sipped tea.

The pair had been working on the radio show for a year. In that year, they had only fought twice. Once when Pele pushed Avery from the top of the tower after seeing what he thought was a mattress and believing that his friend would simply bounce back up. Another time when Avery took a hoax call seriously and informed the entire town of an imminent jellyfish hurricane.

Teal green. The first caller of the night came in. It was a six year old who slept beside the canal and tickled trout.

'First caller! What's your name and where are you from?'

'Shape. The canal.'

'Shape, The Canal, what would you like to say to the listeners?'

A pause and rustling. 'The night is coming,' he said. 'I am seeing very many giant knees. I am hearing voices from above the clouds. They are talking of shampoo and peanuts. Hullaballoo. Shenanigans. They say that. They are saying such things.'

Pele pushed fingers into his mouth to cork a laugh. Avery glared at him. 'What else did the voices say?'

'They are talking always like clocks. They talk about the clocks. They talk about us. They call the clock tosses idiot dumb stuff. They make the squelching sounds. They make sounds like feet in tomato muck. Squelch.'

Pele let out his laughter and Avery jammed an elbow into that open mouth.

*

Casper entered the milk bar to applause and unopened milk cartons shoved between his hands. He remembered what Sixteen had said and ordered his own. He sat on an upturned bucket at the bar, staring through the glass ceiling at the orange sky. Slim fingers of cloud divided it into wide bands. He thought of Diana yelling at him across a dinner table about the voices in the sky. He thought of himself slouching and falling asleep in a bath of ball-size bubbles.

A loud gang kettled him.

'How will you kill it?'

'What will you use?'

'Can you really do it?'

'Should we be hiding?'

'Not now,' he said. 'I'm tired.'

The Vess twins attempted to empty the area around him. 'The Dinosaur Hunter needs personal space,' they chanted. When a space was cleared, the three of them sat and played Yahtzee until Casper got tired of all the eyes, and excused himself, swaying out into the deep orange.

He didn't want to go back to The Cardboard Hill. He didn't want to be alone. He wanted to sit somewhere and panic and drink milk uninterrupted.

The milk bar, the main milk bar, was in The Circle, next to city hall and the mayor's office and the cathedral. There were other bars, in the fringes of Billion. Casper rarely visited them. They made him feel unsafe. They were full of people like him. People who didn't slot in anywhere and had to cling to edges of whatever giant rotating world they were supposed to be existing on.

He walked for an hour through The Confetti District and Little Uganda and Elmbridge, to The Queen's, a bar he'd once hidden in while trying to escape revelers at The Tentacle Festival.

The Queen's was empty except for its barman and Ned Kloot. During his previous visit, the barman had told Casper everything he knew about Ned Kloot. Casper didn't know why. Casper hadn't asked.

Ned had played the pachinko machine beside the woman's toilet door for twelve hours every day for three years. None of the balls he won were ever been exchanged for anything. They were kept in the basement of his house on The Street of Not Sleeping. He was collecting an inheritance for a son that he didn't have. He had a feeling he sometimes described as being 'in his knees' that he definitely did have a son, somewhere, and that one day the son would return, wearing mohair and softly crying.

'You don't look like you looked earlier,' the barman said. 'You look smaller.' He didn't say it in an unfriendly way. He said it like a pat on the arm.

'Um,' Casper said. 'I don't know. The whole town is looking at me.'

'What do you expect? You're the dinosaur hunter and now there are dinosaurs. You've got something to do. A place. You should be glad.'

'I'm not a dinosaur hunter. I never killed a dinosaur.'

The barman clicked off the radio. It had been irritating that night, consisting mostly of the presenters maliciously nicknaming each other after sea mammals. 'You haven't killed a dinosaur *yet*.'

'What if something goes wrong?'

He winked. 'Then everyone will be eaten there will be no one left to blame you.' He turned and filled a pint glass with strawberry milkshake, then set it before Casper and told him to keep his hands out of his pockets. He leaned in. 'If you're worried, you should go see The Dream Nurse. She'll tell you what to expect.'

Casper stared into his glass. He looked up and over the barman's shoulder at a chalkboard filled with cramped handwriting.

Chocolate for dreams of yesterday.

Banana for dreams of today.

Strawberry for dreams of tomorrow.

The barman was right. He needed to go and see The Dream Nurse. She'd be able to tell him whether or not to abort the plan. She could help. She wouldn't help. He couldn't go to The Dream Nurse. It was too complicated. Things between them had never healed. They were standing with their backs to each other on opposite sides of a deep fissure.

But what else?

He drained the glass in one, thanked the barman, nodded at Ned Kloot, and headed toward The Cardboard Hill.

*

'You can't kill a dinosaur. You don't know how.' Kevin scrunched his mouth in anger until his lips became white. Fizika winced. 'Okay, fine, you can kill a dinosaur.'

'I could kill a hundred dinosaurs if I had to.'

'You could kill a million!'

'Don't take that tone with me you idiot goose.'

Fizika raised his palms. 'I'm not taking any tone with anyone.'

'I'm sick of your obnoxious attitude.' Kevin flagged down a waiter in a tabard and ordered another round of sweet teas and a platter of fudge blocks. The waiter dipped his head in a shallow bow and disappeared.

Fizika silently mouthed 'obnoxious attitude?' as though to a camera crew hidden behind the bar.

They were sitting in The Kissing Hall at the edge of Elmbridge. Neither of them had done any kissing. Every time a girl approached, finger outstretched in search of a vacant nostril, Fizika straightened himself expectantly and Kevin made exaggerated shooing motions.

'How are you going to kill it?'

'I'll hit it, obviously.'

'Will that work?'

'I'll hit it hard. And with a bat. I bought a bat.'

'A bat?'

'Yes. Listen, what's wrong with you?'

'But it's going to be a dinosaur.'

Kevin uppercut Fizika in the armpit. 'I know it's going to be a dinosaur. What else is it going to be?'

'I know you know it's going to be a dinosaur.'

'Be quiet.'

Fizika claimed to need the toilet and excused himself. Kevin put his hands beneath his t-shirt and ran his palms over the ridges and bumps and splits. He felt the purple domes of Tatiana-shaped bruises. He pictured himself wearing a T-Rexasaurus head like a glove.

When Fizika returned, there were dribbles of green under each of his nostrils. Kevin snorted but said nothing. His companion had become relaxed and sleepy, slouching almost to the point of sliding from his seat.

'Why do you want to kill it so much? Won't it be dangerous? You should just leave it to that Casper teapot. Relax. Danger for strangers.'

'That isn't what that means.'

'Maybe not.'

'You don't understand anyway.'

'I do. He kissed Tatiana one time. It was an age ago. She won't go back to him just because he kills some dinosaur that probably isn't anywhere anyway.'

'He'll be the richest person in Billion.'

'And she'll leave?' Kevin shrugged and pulled his t-shirt up over his face like a mask. 'Even if you don't like it, he's the dinosaur hunter. It's his job. How would you get there before him?'

Kevin let his t-shirt drop. 'I have a plan.' He dropped a handful of numbers onto the table and left the kissing hall.

*

At home, Casper pulled *A Field Guide to Hunting Dinosaurs* from his pillowcase. He turned to the relevant page and read. He read it again. He pushed his nose against the lines of the drawing. He didn't know why. It wasn't necessary, but he felt like he wanted to pretend to kill it in the right way. The way his father had done. Even though no one would know any different.

*

George Stanza came from a long line of large handed men. His father had been a policeman with fists the size of bowling balls. His father's father had been a policeman with fists the size of boulders. When George was born, with eight fingers and a propensity for accruing bruises from inanimate objects, they bundled him in newspaper and left him on the other side of the town, in an abandoned shipping container that smelled of salt and salmon.

Four and a half years later, under the light of a single candle, George sat in the shipping container, opening and closing his miniature hands like mouths.

'Casper make you rich,' one hand said.

'Mayor make you jail,' the other replied.

'Rich means house.'

'Jail means boring.'

'House means people.'

'Jail means mean people.'

He sighed and stopped. He walked to one corner of the metal room and heaved aside a blue tarpaulin. Admittedly, it did look realistic. Or it at least looked like the pictures George had seen. Felt tip doodles on billboards and illuminated illustrations in old books.

The suit consisted of a giant bamboo frame with black latex

stretched over it. Individual green scales covered it entirely. The eyes were giant marbles. The teeth were shards of glass.

George poked the sleeping dinosaur and made a low humming sound. He climbed into bed and didn't sleep.

*

It's useful to approach the slaying of dinosaurs as a form of puzzle solving. Each kill will require the hunter to complete a series of moves specific to each species. Even within individuals of a species there will be a degree of variance, meaning that the techniques set forth in this manual may need slight alteration.

The T-Rexasaurus is responsible for more known fatalities than all other species of dinosaur combined. Although not the largest of its kind, it houses between four and six hundred glass teeth as well as the ability to run faster than any train, making it a formidable opponent not to be underestimated.

The first stage of the slaying requires getting the beast horizontal, thus rendering it immobile and providing easy access to its head for the second stage. The second stage needs some kind of large, hard-edged object to be dropped into the jaw of the dinosaur. Lastly, the nostrils should be plugged, forcing the T-Rexasaurus to swallow the object, which will then become lodged in its throat, choking it to death.

Good luck.

HAUL ROAD

| RYAN W BRADLEY

Even at twenty-five miles an hour the snowfall looks like a TV left on through dawn. French is on the radio, letting the checkpoint know how fucked the storm is. There's nothing we can do to not end up in a ditch but try to watch what we can see of the road, or worse, the pipeline. Of course, the checkpoint's still timing us, that's the rules and breaking the haul road's speed limit is the kind of thing that'll get you shit-canned.

French hangs the mic on the dash. "Hey, G.P.," he says, picking up where he left off, "how's a Green Peace turd like yourself do with the ladies?"

I fold the map across my legs. Doing twenty-five we're still looking at forty minutes.

"You daydreaming about all that twat?"

"Being a democrat isn't the same as being in Green Peace," I say. "Anyway, what were you guys doing in my wallet?"

"Calm down, Junior. We've got to be careful, in case we got a certified Commie on our crew." French grins big, showing a few holes in his smile. "You're paying enough attention to that clock for the both of us." He taps the green numbers blinking on the radio. "How long you figure?"

"Forty minutes."

"Jesus."

"Could be worse."

"Really?" French turns to me. "So this isn't the first time you've driven the haul road, huh?"

"It is," I say, though French knows as much.

He flings his hand at the windshield, his nails clanking against the glass. "This shit gets people killed."

"What kind of rookies break a fucking drill?"

"Happens to the best of them. Your day will come."

"Bullshit," I say, and French shakes his head.

"Come on, it's a long drive. Tell me about all that fresh-out-of-high-school ass you're getting."

"I've got a girlfriend."

"No joke?"

"Name's Sara."

"Settling down at twenty-two? You really are wet behind the ears. So, how's that going?"

The wipers blur back and forth across the windshield, without a chance of keeping up.

"What'd they do to their drill anyway?"

"Hit too much rebar, I guess. Don't matter," French says, jerking his thumb at the backseat, "we've still got to take them this one. So, she a hot little thing, your girl?"

"Fuck."

"Nevermind. Shit."

"I just don't want to think about it."

"Problems in paradise? Lay it on me, I've lost more women than you've met."

"It's all fucked," I say, tapping my fingers on my knee, a nervous habit that drives Sara nuts.

French is hunched over the steering wheel trying to find the road.

"What could be fucked about twenty-two-year-old pussy?"

"Sara's pregnant."

He doesn't take his eyes off the road, but it feels like he's staring directly at me. "Shit, you got yourself in deep, didn't you?"

"Believe me, I know."

"You don't know a damn thing."

The snow is making me dizzy and I'm glad French is driving.

"Well, you two talked about it or what? How you leaning?"

"Like the Tower of Pisa."

French laughs. "Yeah?" He sits back long enough to shift around a bit before hunching forward again. "When did you find out?"

"Couple weeks ago." My last R&R, two weeks at home, sleeping with Sara, getting drunk at whatever bar we stumbled into, until one night she wanted to stay in. Watch a movie. "She went to a doctor the day before I flew back to Deadhorse." I shove my hands between my thighs.

"Crap way to leave things."

"Definitely."

"What's she think about it all?"

I fix my eyes on the dashboard. "She's Irish Catholic, she wouldn't ever... you know." I still can't believe she didn't slap me just for saying the word.

The radio crackles. "You numb-nuts out there or what? Truck Two-O-Five did you read?"

French picks up. "You going to keep us warm?"

"We weren't getting a response for over five minutes. What's going on?"

"We didn't hear shit from you until now," French says.

"That's not good. You guys need to be checking in like clockwork. How's the road?"

"The road? Fuck off." French slams the receiver back on its dock. "Assholes sitting there at a damn desk. You never want to be one of those guys, G.P., never." He looks at me and I nod. "Those guys with desk jobs, they've forgotten what real work is."

For a second I picture French as my father, that we're driving to Fairbanks or something. Going camping, "Just a boys' weekend," he'd tell my mother. I look at French. I don't know, but I imagine wherever my dad is he's got a full set of teeth.

"I don't think I can do it," I say.

French taps the brakes and we start to fishtail, then skid back on track. He looks at me, his eyes ball bearings, his jaw tight.

"What? You little prick, you're thinking of bailing? Listen, I've got two little girls. Been to jail twice. Compared to anything else this is the sweet life."

"Sure," I say.

He waves his arms at the blizzard. "This, right here, is a goddamn piece of paradise."

"That why everybody talks about saving up for houses in Hawaii or Florida? It's like the goddamn Alaskan state mantra."

He digs into his jeans pocket and pulls out a small metal poker chip. "You know what this is?" he asks, holding it in front of my face.

I shake my head.

"Five years sober. My first meeting was the day my wife told me she was pregnant."

"I'm not a drunk."

"Never said you were."

The only sound is the heater on full blast, and I strain, wondering if I can hear the snow falling.

"Kids happen, G.P.," French says, his voice quieter than before. "People do their best, it's all they can. Your only choice is whether you're going to raise that kid, or puss out."

"I'd be a horrible father," I say.

"Jesus. You can't get a much worse candidate for fatherhood than me, but I got my shit together. I work in this damn Popsicle stand six out of every eight weeks so my wife can be home to take care of our girls."

"I don't know the first thing about being a dad. I'm only twenty-two, you said it yourself."

"I'll say something else, too," French says. "You don't have much choice." He lifts his hat and rubs his forehead.

"There are a lot of choices."

"Name one." French eases on the gas, but doesn't stop. The snow swirls around us. "Got one yet?"

I shake my head. We should be at the checkpoint in less than twenty minutes.

"Two-O-Five, you there?"

French doesn't pick up. He takes his eyes off the road to look at me again.

"Well," I say.

"Truck Two-O-Five. Two-O-Five."

French squeezes the radio with his ash gray fingers. "We're here," he says. "Maybe twenty minutes out."

"Why don't you do the checking in next time? Say ten minutes?"

"Sure thing."

We drive in silence and I strain to see the road. The brim of French's Carhartt hat is touching the windshield. With the heater on, the cab is thick with sweat. The tires slip, slight at first, then the bed of the truck is sideways. We're spinning. I brace one hand on the seat and hold onto the handle above the door with the other.

"Mother-bitch, shit-ass," French says, but it's distant, like I'm a kid eavesdropping from the backseat.

We go off the road with a bump that sends my head into the roof, even with my seatbelt on. French is still pumping on the gas, trying to get us back on track, but we're shit out of luck, and he knows it. The truck lurches as he lets off the pedal and we spit backward into the nothingness beyond the road. Sliding, we tip on our side. My body snaps forward, my hat falling off as I slam into the dashboard. There's a short burst from the horn, French thrown into the wheel. Even though I don't see anything out my window, I know I'm looking at the ground.

French is hanging over me, suspended by his seatbelt. The cab's light is dim and flickering, but I can see his forehead's starting to swell.

"Jesus fuck," he says. "You all right, G.P.?"

I take a deep breath. "Yeah." I can feel the lump growing on my own head, and the burn across my chest from the belt doing its best to hold me still.

"You know what stopped us don't you?"

I nod, but he says it anyway.

"The pipeline."

"How are we going to get out?"

"The only way we can," he says. "My window." He reaches for the crank on the side of his door, rolls the window down. The musty cab chills instantly. "Better pull on your coat."

French shows his missing teeth. I reach below the seat, where I had stuffed my extra gear.

"I'm going to pull myself out, then you can pass me mine."

French grabs the window frame with one hand and undoes his seatbelt with the other. His legs drop in front of my face. I smell the dried mud on the bottom of his Xtra Tuffs. He grunts and pulls himself halfway out of the window.

"Couldn't see a tit out here if it was in your face," he says. "Hand me my shit before I freeze to death."

I unbuckle myself and grab his jacket, wadded up in the backseat. The concrete drill is in two pieces on the floor of the cab. I plant my feet on the door and stand up, reaching French's jacket out the window.

"I think I should take a look around. See if the radio's working."

I hunch down and grab the mic, my hand already so cold it's hard to grip. I hold down the button and am greeted by fuzz.

"This is truck Two-O-Five," I say. "Do you read?" More fuzz. I try again with the same result. "I think it's busted."

"Shit." I hear French push off the frame of the truck. "Snow's over my knees," he says. "Can you get out?"

I zip up my coat, pull on my gloves, and replace my baseball hat with a knit one that I pull over my ears. Reaching both hands out the window, I pull myself up and into the white.

"Drill's broke, too," I say, adjusting so I'm sitting on the door.

"We got enough to worry about. Get down here." French is barely visible until I slide off the truck and land next to him. "We've got to check out the damage around back," he says. "We'll go around the bed until we find the pipeline."

We walk with our hands out, holding onto the truck. I can hear French's breathing ahead of me. He stops and I push between him and the truck. I reach out with my free hand, waiting to touch something solid. When I do, the snow around my legs is stained black and I lean forward. There's a faint glow from the tail lights, and I see the glinting rush.

French taps me on the shoulder, mumbling more cusses. "We can't stay here."

My glove is wet with oil, the familiar smell throws me back to my dad working on his truck in the driveway.

"What choice do we have?"

"The checkpoint can't be far. We've got to find the road." French slaps me on the back and turns around.

I turn my back to the growing pool of black snow and fight through the drift. At the front of the truck, French says if we follow the headlights we'll find the road.

"If the bed's in the pipeline," he says, "the truck must be facing that way." He takes his hand off the hood and pushes on. "Stay close."

"Right behind you," I say, sticking out a hand to touch his back.

The ground slopes upward and I feel gravel under my boots. The snow on the road is only shin high, but my legs feel like I've been running in sand.

"Should I have brought the drill?" I ask, frost budding on my lips.

"Busting the pipeline open, no one's going to be worrying about a drill." French's breathing is growing heavier.

I pull the collar of my coat over my face, yank my hat down tighter. The first day of training they said to report spills of any liquid immediately. I never thought it would be more than a joke to use when someone was dumping the remains of a cup of coffee. But behind us product is spilling at a rate that causes heart attacks for environmentalists and oil tycoons both.

"How far do you think?"

"Not far, G.P." French says.

I can feel his breath heating my cheeks.

"Got to keep warm." He is by my side, putting an arm around my shoulder. He pulls me close, the way a father might.

People get lost in weather like this, everything looking the same, and for a moment I think it wouldn't be so bad to disappear into the tundra. But French wrapping himself around me has got me thinking I would know when a kid needed comfort.

French coughs, spurts of frozen breath cracking the air. "Father-hood's not looking so bad now, is it?"

Though the cold is painful in my lungs, I laugh.

The wind picks up, whips through my jacket and hat, exposing the cracks, tearing at my skin. I focus on feeling the road underfoot, tell myself we're still on gravel. In front of us is a blank canvas, an empty field of white. I stare ahead against the wind and snow, begging my eyes to be tricked into seeing the yellow light of a lantern, showing the way.

GLORIA
| KIRSTEN ALENE

No birds sing in this part of the forest. There is no sound of rollicking wildlife, no shivering undergrowth. No wind moves the dark leaves of the canopy. No fresh air at all has penetrated this part of the forest and what air manages to squeeze itself through the heavy branches and graying pine needles is gelatinous and difficult to breathe.

Laboring with the stagnant atmosphere, his feet disturbing little plumes of tree dust and brittle four-autumns-past leaves, is a man with the pinched expression of a starving jackal and the neck of a sickly, colorless giraffe. The man puzzles over a tree, moves on to a bush, then across a small clearing to another tree. No great light is coming down through the trees, though it is a cloudless day, and his jackal features are only as obvious as the vague, shallow lines of split bark on the beech trees he grazes with anxious fingers.

Years ago, each tree and bush seemed distinctive and unique. The character of the plant life radiated out of each separate needle, forming a pathway from the road where he has parked his decrepit CRV, to the familiar grounds of his youthful wanderings. He is aggravated by the absolute sameness of this once distinct foliage. But he is also relieved. His fierce canine expression slackens and his face returns to its customary calm. Head wavering on his prodigious, pale neck, he puffs out his cheeks and blows a raspberry in the silence.

If any of those cohorts from his youth—the ones who knew, as he once knew, the tight and claustrophobic inches of the forest like the backs of their hands—could see him now, he would have been a stranger. They would, however, despite the unkind effect of the years that separated them from him currently, have most definitely recognized his previous jackal-like expression. A look like that is unforgettable.

Fortunately for him, all of those people who might once have been able to identify him, all of those people who knew the forest once, who knew him once, are gone. No one has a chance of navigating the deepness of this forest. No one except Steven.

***

Tree shadows have followed him as he speeds down the wet highway, cutting a line from the Mackley Park turn-off through a haze of thin rain and a half-hearted fog straight to the bedside of his father-in-law.

***

"Dennis, she looks up at me every day. She looks up through that moss when I call her. You don't know how cold her eyes are now."

Dennis's father-in-law, Steven, has been cloistered in the Lakewood Valley Assisted Living Facility since the age of twenty-seven. Steven suffers from an intense and debilitating paranoia that surfaced in his youth. His madness culminated in a string of arsons, for which he was arrested. When he admitted to his legal counsel that a sinister man who had been following him forced him to burn the houses, he was deemed incapable of governing himself, and implanted in the home.

Despite this seemingly insurmountable handicap, Steven has dedicated himself to the study of science and natural philosophy. Years ago, Dennis's visits to the private apartment in Lakewood were like free tutelage. Steven's wise and lonely ramblings, interrupted only occasionally by fits of oblique terror and rage, were Dennis's only stimulation in a world now devoid of the rages and terrors he had himself known as a youth.

When true and honest madness began to manifest in Steven it took weeks for Dennis to notice. Now it is difficult to discern any remainder of the former man in a steaming pool of insanity. Only once every few visits does some clairvoyant and beneficent pronouncement make its way past his father-in-law's cracked, trembling lips revealing that a man is sequestered within, as the mad man which houses him is sequestered in the Facility.

Dennis no longer bothers to knock on the apartment door, the stoop of which is overgrown with tangles of morning glory vine and slick with the pulpy remains of twenty or thirty newspapers. Slipping in the newspaper puddle and cursing the neglectful staff, Dennis shoulders the door open and steps inside. The whole apartment smells of medical supplies and dampness. There is probably mold growing in the walls. Mold abounds here, in this complex, and in the town. Every man-made structure is its sporing ground, every dark place its little chapel. Covering his nose and mouth with the sleeve of his jacket as he passes the filthy, cramped restroom, Dennis walks straight across the bedroom to the window. "Steve, it's so muggy in here, you tell them to open the window when they come." He shoves open the high window which shudders as it moves in its uneven aluminum frame.

His father-in-law lays prostrate on the bed, strapped down beneath soft, beige sheets, breathing heavily into his pillow. Dennis takes a seat near the bed, in a rickety folding chair that has almost grown into the worn carpet. Steven moves his head left and right. The creases in his neck and face stretch into faint lines, then fold back into papery, elephant skin. Outside the window, children scream and laugh. A gunshot rings out far off in the distance, somewhere in the forest near where Dennis recently wandered.

"I didn't want to tell you, Dennis but I'm in love." Dennis reaches out to hold the withered fingers in their cotton-lined cuff. "I'm in love with her, I have been for years. She comes in here to see me. I never leave, you see. I can't." The hand jerks away at Dennis's touch. The whole bed jumps as the strap pulls at the bed frame. "I'm in love, don't you get it? Can't you comprehend you ignorant, fascist swine. You limaceous endomorph, you zeophyte, you placenta." Steven yells angrily for a moment and is calm. Dennis's eyes unfocus, the whole room is a beige, antiseptic blur. The bed is a raft, the children peering in through the window, holding themselves up by their elbows, are trying to get a good look through boiling waves of brownness. With his eyes squinted up and strained, they look like dogs, their jaws slavering, eyes wide and pupil-less. Other gunshots ring out, some closer, some farther up the mountainside. Old men out hunting the coyotes with their sons. Dragging huge, rotten carcasses through the undergrowth to leave the scent of death behind them.

"I went there just yesterday, Dennis," Steven says, suddenly cogent and bright-eyed. He snatches Dennis's hand and grips it tightly. "The nurse who comes here, she's a witch. She leaves my bonds loose so I can slip right out. I think she pities me. She's a whore, too, I've seen her. I followed her to the spot. You know the spot I'm talking about. Right?

You know. They all know." The children cackle from the window. Dennis wants to shoo them away, to rise and show them that he is not a corpse, but Steven continues, "I went there to see her. I owed her that much for never speaking. She was so beautiful. She was so thin. She was so damn cold. I know now why you told me…something like that can weigh on a man, I know. I know now. Aren't you glad?"

Dennis nods. He is not glad. He does not like those children hearing this revelation, however insane and disjointed it may sound. He rises from the chair but before he can make a movement for the window, they have yelped and retreated. A moment passes and they resume their game out of sight. Another gunshot.

***

People seem more concerned when a body blossoms in roadside foliage, than when it sinks and fails to resurface. In one version of events, the failure of the body to resurface was proof of her immediate ascension.

***

In the kitchen, surrounded by his wife's collection of ceramic roosters and a wide expanse of busy rooster-themed wallpaper, Dennis jabs his fork into a potato. He imagines the potato screaming, writhing beneath his powerful incisions.

"Daddy?" Dennis jabs again, prying apart the papery brown skin to reveal the flaky, pulsing flesh beneath. A cloud of steam breaks over his face. "Daddy? Are you okay?"

"Dennis, stop violating that potato and eat your dinner before I take it away." Nothing aggravates Dennis more than when his wife addresses him like a child. She has no business talking like that to him, or to anyone. Gloria is far past needing to be threatened and chastised. Not that she ever needed discipline.

His daughter smiles at him and puts her soft hand on top of his. Dennis's wife clicks her tongue disapprovingly. "What's up?" Gloria says. She is the most beautiful child he has ever seen. At the age of five, they had thought she could never be prettier but she has only grown more stunning in the decade since, her face blossoming around the twin anther of her radiant brown eyes like a real bayou lily. Her beauty is complimented by a single dimple in her left cheek, a square but not masculine chin, a lineless and peach-smooth forehead, and an untamable head of perfect golden curls which are now pinned up in a light cascade by a little silver headband. Now, as is happening with increasing frequency, she looks more like her namesake than her mother or her father. More like her namesake than any other living being. Dennis's skin twitches involuntarily and his wife snaps, "I mean it, Dennis.

What was the story about the woman intellectual, the succubus who poisoned her husband's second wife with two drops of her corpse cold blood? Did that blood penetrate the fertile womb of the innocent, ignorant female? Was the resultant child angelic or demonic?

Dennis, ignoring his wife's persistent disapproving babble, grips his daughter's hand and pats it lovingly. "Nothing's wrong, sweetheart. I was just thinking about your grandpa." Dennis observes his wife stiffen slightly. She has not seen her father in four years. The last visit was so painful and humiliating that she has refused to continue seeing him. I'd rather, she says, remember him as a real person than a skeleton spewing nonsense and insults to an empty room. She hates that Dennis sees him, hates when Dennis mentions him, most of all she hates when Dennis talks about him in front of Gloria. Her grey eyes grow steely and dark. Gloria smiles sadly and nods, as if she understands. As if her huge, reflective eyes house as deep a vat of sadness as they sometimes appear to house.

When Gloria has been installed in her bed and kissed by both her father and mother, Dennis's wife pours a tremendous glass of whiskey and hands it to her husband. "Thanks, Kat."

They sit in the living room in silence, trees outside the large bay window barely illuminated by a sliver of a moon, thick branches unsuccessfully muffling the continued sound of gunshots on the mountainside. "Still hunting?" Kat says in response.

"I guess it's the only way to be sure," Dennis says, heaving himself to his feet to peer out the window into what he knows is just complete darkness. "I was out there today, but I didn't hear anything," he mutters mostly to himself but Kat, nose in her own glass, hears him and snorts.

"You were what?"

"I was out, you know, where we used to go."

"I hope by 'we' you don't think you are referring to myself, Dennis." Hidden by an overwhelming amount of disdain is a hint of fear.

"No, dearest, I was not referring to you."

Among the glassy reflection of roosters, he can just make out the small flashes of light from rifles firing in the dark, separated from their cracking reports by full seconds, two seconds sometimes three.

***

They almost lived there, out in the woods. Which is foolish. There is more mold there, more rank decay and stagnant water than anywhere else in the town. It is infested. It is filthy.

But to them, it felt open and clean.

Boys in masks and costumes flee through the brush, their capes and shoelaces tangling in nettles and blackberry bushes, spores suck down into their lungs as they struggle with the undergrowth while he watches.

***

In one version of events she is alone in her room at the top of the stairs, looking out into the garden when a moon god with heaving chest and naked limbs slithers out of the hedge and in one swift movement, mounts the rose trellis and knocks on the glass of her window. When she wakes, she leaves with him and never creeps back down the stairs again.

***

When Dennis wakes next to his wife, his immediate reaction is to recoil. Two huge, intently staring black eyes have replaced her small, watery grey ones which, in the morning, are usually squinted with sleepiness and slightly grumpy. The momentum of his initial recoil sends him out of the bed and onto the floor where he lands, legs tangled into an immovable knot of sheets. His breath comes in short gasps as he fights with his feet, waiting for the alien face to peer over the side of the bed but no face appears, which terrifies him more. After a minute of silent struggle, Kat's familiar groggy face slides into view. She laughs. "Were you awake?" Dennis asks, his heart pounding.

"I am now, geez, what did you do?"

Dennis watches his daughter back the car down the driveway. When she reaches the end he goes to meet her, pulls open the heavy driver's side door and pats her head. "You're getting better."

She looks at him very seriously. "You don't have to worry. Everything will be alright, you'll see."

More gunshots echo faintly through the valley.

Dennis pulls into the parking lot of the town's only bar and sits in his car for a while. Eating breakfast here alone is better than enduring his wife's moans and wails about the various chores and tasks he has neglected over soggy bacon, dry eggs, and stale toast at home.

"They're really going after the Keye-Oats, huh?" a filthy, plaid-shirted man says at the next booth. His friend stirs a small dish of mayonnaise slowly with a French fry, "'Spose," he responds.

"But then what can they do? It's the only real way to be sure."

His friend grunts and continues stirring the mayonnaise.

"You know what they say when some animal gets a taste for human flesh?"

The friend's blank stare focuses a little and he pulls the fry out of the mayonnaise. He places the fry delicately between his lips and sucks off the mayonnaise before dipping it back into the dish.

"I read some about these tigers in Bombay all ganged up, kilt four hundred people and the natives had to go and call this English hunter name of Laney. He took care of that bitch. Was sick, they said. Something went wrong with it."

The friend grunts again, "Ain't nothing wrong with a Keye-Oat been eatin' babies. In their blood, isn't it. Scavagers."

"You mean scavengers."

"What I said. Nothing wrong."

The first man shakes his head. "You listen here, I'll show you something ain't wrong. You come see what Bill's boy brought in last night. Not no damn Keye-Oat, I can tell you."

The friend drags the fry out of the mayonnaise again and sucks it clean. The fry sags down. He lets it fall onto a plate of untouched chicken fried steak and country potatoes.

***

"When she rose up, all phantom like and bleeding out from every orifice as if her death was as fresh as a minute ago, I think I shat myself but then it was calm. I saw her bleeding for what it was and I can tell you, it was nothing dangerous or premonitory. It was like a tribute." Steven lay back on his pillow and sighed deeply. "I can tell you now just how I found her, you'll be interested, I know. She's hidden well, but there are certain distinguishing features along the path. A knotted branch, a fern that's bent and growing up the side of a beech tree, a lot of moss hanging down one side of a boulder, and some beetles rolling dung along a well worn path in the dirt. A circle of mushrooms, a break in the trees where a ray of light shines down and there, she's just sitting there quiet."

Dennis scratches his forehead. He can hear the gunshots better from here. A myriad of companion sounds drift in through the barred window: bird calls, the whoops of hunters, the yelps of dogs grazed by bullets. Once sharper than a Fennec Fox's, Dennis ears ping only dully with each successive gunshot. He swallows back panic as Steven turns cataract-speckled eyes on him. "They're so far out in the forest, Dennis."

Dennis gulps again, rearranges the chair so he isn't facing Steven and says, "I know."

"No one ever goes that far out into the forest, Dennis."

In one version of events, he watches her soundlessly from the exaggerated afternoon shadow of a lone gas pump as she clambers up the steep sharp steps of a bus, clutching a single valise at the bottom of her stomach, thinking she is alone at last, feeling as if she is being watched. Comforted by those invisible eyes like they are the eyes of someone wise and eternal.

***

It has long been the case that those closest to the wild fear the wild the most. It's like being in a flood zone. Five miles away from the river, the inevitable flooding seems innocuous. The house is on stilts, you have flood insurance and a canoe. All of your valuables are on the second floor. The children know how to swim. You confront the terror of your world being washed in silty river water with preparedness and calm, every six or seven months, by waxing the canoe and sealing things in Ziploc bags.

When you are eleven feet from the river, you confront the inevitable possibility of flood when you wake to hear the waves lapping on the banks, when you are weeding the garden, when you are making lunch in the kitchen watching the rushing spring snow melt edge up the shore, lap over the sides of the levy, trickle onto the driveway.

Flooding seems much more of a threat when the water is visible from your bedroom window.

This is why Dennis lives in the center of town. Although wilderness surrounds him, he can't hear it lapping at the banks as well as he used to.

***

Gloria stands with a stick in her hand on the top of a pile of rocks downstream from the elementary school. Her hair is braided high on her head, her cheeks are pink and vaguely freckly. Her eyes are narrowed into a squint.

She is angry with her mother. Her mother doesn't understand her. Her mother doesn't understand anything. Her mother doesn't even understand her father. Her mother seems like not her mother. She kicks a rock into the river. It bounces on the shallow bottom and pops back up before coming to rest in a deep pool where a small fish bolts away from it, scuttling straight out into the current where it is swept up and out of sight. Gloria wants to read in her room. She wants to back the car down the driveway every day and make breakfast before school. She is smart enough to know what her mother means when she says: "Go find a young boy." She is not dumb. She will find a young boy the way other girls find young boys. She will find a young boy for her mother.

Just as she was thinking this thought, a boy wielding a stick similar to her own emerges from the tangle of blackberry bushes on the opposite bank. Her first reaction is to think, "Oh boy, it must hurt to walk through all of those prickly bushes," but this thought is immediately followed by another: "Oh, here we are."

The boy is shirtless and brown, from dirt or sun it is impossible to tell. Gloria waves to him: "Hey, hey!" but he doesn't turn to look at her. He is looking upstream, toward the soccer fields of the school on her side of the river. Another boy emerges from the bushes beside him, wearing a black mask and a cape. Soon a third boy and a fourth have joined the first two, one with a horse mask, the other a plastic axe. Gloria waves again, throws a rock into the bushes, and slides down to the water's edge. "Hey!"

None of the boys turn. Gloria thinks a moment, she examines her clothes, unbuttons her blouse, and hikes her pink denim skirt all the way up to her rib cage. There we go, she thinks. "Hey!" They stare blankly in the direction of the soccer fields. Gloria can't see what they are staring at from down on the bank, but she doesn't think she can climb all the way back up. Instead she takes off her shoes and wades out into the water, which is freezing. Feet numbed, she steps out farther. The bottom of the river is soft and slippery. Her left foot slides down one rock and lands with a crack on another. A little translucent cloud of blood blossoms up into the water and is swept off by the current until only a small red thread of fluid trickles out of her heel. It doesn't hurt, so she continues on. The number of boys has grown while she was struggling across the river. There are seven now on the opposite bank. They are watching her now. One of them is laughing, but the rest look sympathetic. She scowls at them and clambers up the steep opposite bank, clutching at blackberry bushes to drag herself up.

A boy with dog ears and a fake plastic nose bends down and offers her a hand. He hoists her up through the blackberries, which drag at her clothes and the skin of her legs. It feels like a bad sunburn. Then before the dog boy has put her on her feet, they take off running in a pack. Gloria is not her PE teacher's favorite student for nothing, though, and she sprints after them.

**

He is glad when the sounds of gunshots and stomping boots do not carry into the heart of the forest. He feels waves of pressure standing in the claustrophobic silence as panic and frustration swell in his chest. He will never find it, which is distressing. No one will ever find it, which is comforting. His father-in-law has already found it, which is…impossible.

The road is slicker than usual. Dennis can feel the wheels slipping beneath him, no traction on the turns. And he keeps seeing bright yellow eyes in the foliage at the side of the road. It is unnerving. They are everywhere, like they say. Maybe those men are right to be out here shooting them. There is obviously some sort of infestation.

Ten miles from the Mackley Park turn-off, he rolls down the window and slows to a crawl. Rain is pinging off the glass and the hood, sizzling slightly as it hits the hot metal. He strains his ears to hear beyond the engine and the tinny sound of rain. A thunderous howling echoes off the sides of the mountain. Thousands of them, still. It is getting dark.

***

In one version of events, he kills her in the forest, leaving her ripe and swelling body naked in the crook of a tree, legs spread to birth into the shadowed and featureless forest an endless series of plagues and pestilences.

***

Gloria realizes she is falling behind. Her slashed heel starts to sting. Her thorn-whipped legs and arms burn, her sweaty face is beet red and puffy from panting for breath as they bolt up through hills so steep they have to climb on all fours to stay upright. She can still see Dog Ears in the distance, his bare feet kicking up sticks, moss and dirt as he hops through the trees. She is on her knees, one elbow on the ground. Her mother is probably worried; her father will be getting home soon. It seems like a good idea to turn back and it is obvious at this point that she will not be getting any action from these fellows.

Someone at the front stops and turns around. It is Horse Mask. He might be looking at her, although it is hard to tell where his eyes are pointing underneath the mask. She stands up. "I'm leaving, this isn't fun." She turns, hoping to make a dramatic exit, but she slips on the hill and skids down several yards on her back. A sound of murmuring grows louder as Dog Ears and another boy clamber after her, sliding through the leaves like snakes.

They grab her arms, one under each elbow, and hoist her up between them. At this distance, they seem much smaller than they did and she is embarrassed. She tries to pull down her skirt a little, to cover her muddy thighs but they are gripping her too tightly and she cannot get her arms free. She writhes and struggles but their small hands are vice-grips, tightening like Chinese finger traps as she struggles.

***

"Your daughter is at Amelia's for the weekend," Kim says without turning as Dennis enters the kitchen. Something unidentifiable is boiling on the stovetop, a sort of greenish paste. Dennis peers into the pot for as long as he can stand before hoisting himself up onto the counter.

"Don't sit on the counter, Dennis," his wife snaps. He slides off. There is a moment of silence then she says, "If it wasn't just down the street, I'd…" she shakes her head. Kim spends most of her life shaking her head. "I spent all day at Michael and Karen's and you won't believe what the boys have been dragging in off the mountain."

Dennis grunts, picks at the lip of the counter.

"Don't pick at that." Dennis curls his fingers into his palm. "Those animals are so thick up there you can shoot blind and kill twenty. That's what they're saying." Dennis scoffs.

His wife scowls, seems disappointed.

Dennis reaches out a hand to touch her shoulder and she whips it away, splattering the wall with green goop from the stove. "Damn it!" His wife's face mutates once again into the black-eyed, pupil-less mask he has seen before. And he knows what is going on.

***

They are climbing up. The hill steepens under their feet. Gloria's white tennis shoes are streaked with sap and mud. Young boys float effortlessly over the wasting pine needles around her, ducking in and out of sight, a constantly shifting swarm of masked faces and torn clothing.

As they climb they become more ghoulish. They become whiter as darkness drops down over the mountain. Gunshots crack in Gloria's ears. Up ahead, a glimmer of light like a hearth fire.

***

Dennis picks his way through the foot-deep pulp of decayed newspapers like a gazelle. The door, slick and wet, stands slightly ajar and he pushes it open, wondering if one of the nurses is changing the sheets, dreading the sight of pale grey slacks stretched to amazing proportions by the giant backside of an old nurse. His father-in-law is in love with one of the nurses. Dennis can never remember which one. The man has loved her from the first day. Until the madness set in, she was his one obsession. A voice murmurs in the bedroom as Dennis turns the corner and steps over the carpet sticky and stiff with dried urine and mildew. But when Dennis nudges the door open with the tip of one finger no one is in the room.

"You take her by the hand and lead her to the woods. You take her to the place you knew you all would go. You lie her down and worship her. You take her by the hand and lead her there," the voice whispers

Dennis's feet seem locked to the floor. He tries to move, to run, to look around but all he can do is stiffen more. He has lost control of all his muscles. He nearly shits himself before his weakened ears finally hone in on the source of the sound and his feet carry him, breathless, to the window. Under the sill, in the cool sand beside the apartment wall, a small boy with half a Barbie and half a bologna sandwich sits whispering to the sandwich. The Barbie is bottom-less, a pen puncture through one eye. As Dennis watches from the empty bedroom of his father-in-law, the boy stabs the Barbie with a penknife and whirls around to stare at Dennis.

He hisses like a cat through the false plastic beak of a black bird. Then he runs, leaving the sandwich and the Barbie behind.

***

"Dad?"

***

"There's a place, son, out back of these woods, far past the other side of this mountain, all that was south as south as south goes, all downhill, all clear and washed out by fire underneath the trees. In that place a flower grows that'll only bloom when it gets a breath of fire. The seeds lie dormant until the winds bring the scent of flame and then they start to grow up, up, up. The seven plagues all come from the bloated belly of one pregnant bitch, son and that bitch is the earth. The hellish blossom comes and it sweeps across the ground like its own wave of wildfire. Devouring everything that remains. Then in the night its seeds drop into the lush bed of its smothering leaves and they grow swaddled in the warm organic heat of their mother. And when they're big enough, they come for you. They come for you so hard."

***

Kim's eyes dart from fire to fire, unfocused, looking through the reflection, almost opaque with roosters crowding the furniture in the living room. Her dining room expands into the night, it stretches out parallel to the house, all the way to the mountain where sparks ignite and die, ignite and die. Her child is safe in the kitchen of another mother. Kim imagines her child in the fires, in the night in a vision so vivid and pure that it might be clairvoyance. She gasps and smiles. She chuckles to herself.

***

Dennis is speeding up the mountain in pursuit of his ancient and demented father-in-law when a blue heron swoops low in front of his windshield. The antennae of the car nicks the birds tremendous wing and it crumples mid-flight, into a diminished heap on the side of the highway. Dennis slams on his breaks and backs up. He watches in the rear-view mirror as the bird is smothered in the blackness of night. Then the night around the bird shimmers and the blue heron is covered in black birds.

***

"Where are you my good, sweet girl? Where are you? You led me to your home so many nights, so many nights I followed you while you dreamt and now where are you? My feet are old, I only have a minute and I'm so cold now. Come on and find me, lead me where you know we all must go."

***

The boys are skeletons now. Skeletons in plastic masks and overalls so grave-tattered they could be ancient sail cloth or loose thread, they shudder with rasping breath after rasping breath, into the empty body cavity, out of the muscle-less larynx, into the empty body cavity.

"Children…"

Gloria shivers in her pink denim skirt and modest cotton bra. Her hair has become the home of four beetles and a white moth, which has mistaken her shimmering golden strands for the winding beams of the moon. The skeleton boys throw her down before a woman who looks very familiar. The woman is breathing through her teeth and alternately gasping and moaning as if in the middle of amazing and invisible intercourse. Beside her is a backpack filled with fruit so molded and mushy that it is only distinguishable by the overpowering smell and a swarm of flies that surround it.

"Children…"

Gloria recognizes the woman. She knows the woman.

Gloria throws up suddenly. Her vomit is warm and pink. The woman is Gloria. Gloria is hugely pregnant, her mouth is wet and black. She is tied to the base of a tree with a bungee cord that has cut through the fat of her belly to the muscle beneath. The wound is festering.

Gloria's legs are spread wide and something is crowning. Gloria is staring as something red, vein-speckled and hot steams out of her.

She is screaming. The skeleton boys are rasping skeleton laughter.

The thing crowning is blacker than the night.

***

When the blackbirds clear, the heron is a collection of small, hollow bones and a single black eye more doleful and sad than any eye still socketed.

"Dad!" Dennis cries into the forest. "Dad! Steve! Steven!" He struggles to listen but the sound of repeated gunfire is almost deafening. Gunfire and howling.

***

"You have been giving birth for so long, my sweet child. You have been growing them up inside you for a thousand years. Finally, here they come." Steve rubs his graying hands together, trying to feel the creases and the knuckles again but all he feels is like a few soft mittens, formless and textureless. She is not answering. She is not calling back to him when he calls out. Only coyotes are calling back. He pauses. He thinks. Of course. Only the coyotes are calling back. He sprints into the underbrush toward the howling.

***

When her grandfather appears beside her, Gloria is alone with Gloria. She is heaving and panting again. The skeletons have all lain down around her like suckling piglets. They slowly rub their small plastic faces up and down her round hot belly.

He kneels but Gloria is too afraid to look at him and then the crowning head rips through the cervix in a shower of afterbirth. It is a blackbird and it is followed by another. And another. And another.

***

Dennis sits on the curb at the entrance to the Mackley Park trail. A man and his two sons are dragging an animal the size of a moose across the parking lot. The hide is completely stripped away already, huge chunks of meat tear off as they paint a red carpet to their jeep. They heave the creature onto the roof with a system of levers and pulleys already in place and drive off, blood and tissue careening off the back of the Jeep, taken up by the wind and scattered back into the woods where eyes and tongues examine it closely.

The carpet of blood stretches up into the forest, blanketing the path that the body has cleared in the undergrowth.

***

"Find yourself a man, Gloria, find yourself a nice young boy to occupy your time. Put on that short skirt and get the hell out of the house."

***

A swarm of black birds is bursting from Gloria as Steven and Gloria watch. She is stiller than stone and as cold as a corpse. Steven is kneeling, arms outstretched before the swarm when Gloria stands, silhouetted, almost naked and pale before the snowstorm of black feathers. And her father is coming through the trees quite suddenly. He is running, loping up the hill like a jackal on thin legs, his face the menacing grimace Gloria sees in her nightmares. He is clutching a kitchen knife in one hand, a rope in the other.

He says nothing as he deftly plunges the kitchen knife between the ribs of Gloria. When she falls, the scene her body obscured is visible in the half-light. Steven kneels. Gloria is black-lipped, birthing a horde of blackbirds, which speed up, out of the womb, into a tornado in the sky ripping through the forest canopy. Coyotes are scattering. All beasts are scattering in the dimness.

Dennis kneels near his daughter and cradles her head as Steven sings and cries and the blackbirds twirl past them, straight up into the sky.

THE INSTALLATION OF ACTIONS
| BRIAN OLIU

C:\>

C:\> o.exe

Welcome to the O self-extracting executable!

Run install file upon extraction? (Y/N)

Y

Extracting...

If you could believe that this is how it begins, with extraction.
If you could believe that this is how it begins with the forcing
of large seeds spit from a core, the pulling up of a sun from stone,
water from stone, fire from stone, mountains, invisible lines formed
by trompe l'oeil, the pulling out of a god from the head of a god
that was pulled out of chaos, of nothing and everything,
of swirling lines of the antithetical concept and conception
of the cosmos, to pull from the primal emptiness of a black
or green screen something beyond the constraints of white or green
glyphs on a page, pulsating doting dots and victimless time.
If you could believe that this is how it begins,
with a key to the complex causality of events,
that this is a deterministic system that hides between
swings of fate's blade and the inevitable decompression of a series
of items meant to exist beyond what is presented and what exists
somewhere, in the end-user, in the cryptovirologist, in O, in you,
in O, in you. If you could believe that on November 22 1982

the first payload hit somewhere in a grey photographed hospital room
that was never photographed, no cameras,
despite aunts quitting jobs behind checkout scanners,
despite aunts who constantly feel the need to document, printscrn,
kiss the world on its fat cheek and leave a lipstick mark for those to see
later, to be placed in mahogany frames leading up staircases,
to be placed near the top step to represent the first, watching the
descent and passing through time with each step on carpet runner,
watching faces and ties of yesterdays instead of slippery feet flipping
children over until landing on the landing with one sock off
and a welt the size of a diagram of a favorite planet,
the lump reminding you, us, of a breached child being pulled out
by its arm, shredding nerves and making the body forget the twist
or the curl on the right-side. If you could believe
that there were no cameras, no mark of what occurred
and what is about to occur, you would be right to fear the placing
of smaller items into folds and folders,
you would be right to fear the process. If you could believe that it would
all be ruined somehow, either through force or through cataloging,
then you would believe this, all of this to carry some weight of truth,
some heft beyond the carrying of rust and growth and overgrowth
of years spent absorbing things outside yet inside; something both larger
 and smaller than one's self. This is how technology and you and I
and there have drifted; the desire to put more into smaller things,
to crunch, crush, and raster in search for a resolution, the spreading of air,
plates both tectonic and served at meals where we would sit across from
each other or at a right angle, water glasses filled with reckless abandon
like storms in water glasses, teacups, even,
though the water encompassed by glass was not heated, cold,
cold from a cold sink, processed from water elsewhere,
plants elsewhere, and brought here, cold. We crash
our crystal-capsized ships together, ringing true like it once was, delicately.
We guide the water away from our lungs to our bellies where we warm,
absorb. We remember this, not the water, not the process,
but the future we promised in the past, and how we got from there
to here, to elsewhere, to here, where elsewhere is.
So sing, toast to me of the man, Muse, the man of twists and turns

driven time and again off course by time and again like failed circuits
with no stops. But he could not save all things prior and ultra
from disaster, hard as he strove—
the recklessness of old ways, bloated processes
filled with starts never begun.

Sing? (Y/N) Y

And when you die, after the oboloi, they will ask you one question.

C:\>

C:\>dir

Volume in drive C is Brian Oliu
Volume Serial Number is 2211-20E6

Directory of C:\

11/22/1982 10:30a   821,122,110 1.EXE

1 File(s)   821,122,125 bytes
1 Dir(s)   2,672,475,935 bytes free

C:\>1.exe

Someone, somewhere, missed you. When viewing time as a number, it
seems small; to see the number 4071, one has to think if this date has
occurred as of yet, which it has not. When we see a number such as
1982, we automatically ascribe a date to it; it will never function as the
amount of low and high-backed chairs, filled with black fingernailed
men awaiting ripped meat and sex, their hands outreached as water is
poured over them. We see transportation in an unlucky city implode
through the air and across thick flat ground on the same morning. We
see the day nine planets align on the same side of the sun. We see days
bring more of these things, the alignment of things and the misalign-
ment of others, as we see the importance of planets, circles that we

are sorry for, the awareness of life only after cutting us in half near the trunk, counting out then in, in then out to go over the miscounting of orbits, years skipped over and forgotten as the lines in the cross-section blur, lateral meristems feeding on each other, a thousand plateaus as we become arborescent. The opacity of smoke decreases with every swirl as the plane of immanence cuts emits matter in random motion, numbers projected onto screens in front of lovers and men with their shoes off and ice melting inside and out, counting down patterns of distance underneath a child's toy avatar earned solely from being young. But remember the numbers, remember that if you set the refraction of light, things, whatever to a certain level of thinness, thickness, (height not important if x is equal to x, the endless of trajectory of things, wheels) this is where I will be; bright red dawn too obvious, certainly, but slow-moving, much slower than I perceive to be. I am furious violent coming in like a quickness, like an uncommon cold, virus, like the dry scratch at the back of mouths after falling asleep, head against plastic against doubled plastic against air never touched by human hands or converted to waste by human lunges and lungs. I must start somewhere and end elsewhere, the idea of me fading into nothing is something never considered, to spread and dissolve like trails of white, like aspirin in the bottom of an illegal plastic bottle, yet with no fizz of foam or a changing of the make-up of the substance submerged in. All of this permanence brings me to you, an end-stop of end-stops, man in a blue suit with gold tassels and a voice on the other end. At some point you blink as I enter open wounds, subject to visions of scant things and all sins that come from sight, the necessity to see green dials spinning (or so I've heard, I have none of your training or your rewards, her), to see which switch to flip when instinct isn't part of an or the equation, to see rose red dawn rising just before the hours come in sixteens caused by rain and diluted fuel. I can see for a second what you have planned, what words you love to lick off of her tongue, long Os and the father-bother merger, what anger there is at process and how this whole thing works, the unlikeliness of getting from x to x to y in less time than seems possible, an hour lost here, a day lost there. This, this here is proof that I can do it faster, and you, you envy me. You turn away turn to her and turn me in before she remembers I'm gone.

C:\>1.exe -p

Someone, elsewhere, misses you. But believe that this is not their story. Someone, elsewhere, doesn't miss you at all. But believe that this is not their story either. Someone, elsewhere, is fighting for your good name, saying the right things at cookouts and catch-up sessions at salad bars between old friends, knowing that you're gone without being reminded by the mention of your name, telling stories of dark-wooden land-locked islands with the hopes that a daughter of Atlas keeps your belly full with pork and your good heart spellbound. Elsewhere, all is settled. After the wars and waves, children are being born, the combination of blood and fat, images from inside wombs of women who took showers directly above you, bell voices hitting notes of divinity, songs performed at late Sunday church services, long after extended mornings of dehydration and the failure of globe artichoke remedies, we all sing along. Perhaps this is why I am lost; the shrinking away of the central brain from the skull, the rejection of security and the loss of all water, tongue dried out and lifeless with the inability to sing of sacrifice, the guilt of not being able to face the sun and sundresses and to dip my hands in the purification process. Perhaps this is why, elsewhere, I am suspended in what I have expelled; wishing the yellow-toned child seen through remote procedure dryness soon.

Someone, elsewhere, is trying to find you. This was formerly and formally done prior with BackRubs, before equations of 10 to the 100th changed our viewpoint on things, I the 1 in front of a hundred zeroes. Nothing has changed since then aside from voices pitch-shifted and auto-tuned to more solid sounds than you once recognized them when they taunted you from afar, soiled the name of both you and your father and your father's father, (I recognize the cluster of vowels is not easy to pronounce, the tongue hoping for the repetition of an "O" rather than the curling purr of a "U"), the jumbling of letters, the terror in anything foreign or non-Corsican, because home is the garden state, after all, and these are the sons and daughters of tomatoes and basil, where Verrazano-Hudson marriage announcements make back pages of newspapers next to the fat faces of small children and dead investment bankers who moved to the area in the late 1960s, long before I was lost and long before someone tried to find me, first through police blotters and drug charges, then various states of morning dress through limerence. Names and memories of lost causes are surrounded with quotation marks as if instead of requesting to search for all of the items within the punctuation, it is something muttered under breath, my name, Brian Oliu, becoming quotable as if it were an expression of self-doubt only understood within the confines of inverted commas. On days on which I appear forgotten by the Gods, I am found in small pieces; a jumble of words here, an automated message there come clear through the deepweb, memories of me breaking noses in cafeteria lines or failing gymnasium endurance tests, cupcakes on birthdays, invasive surgeries, STOP

Enough. Tell me about yourself now, clearly, point by point. Who are you? Where are you from? Your City? Your Parents? What sort of vessel brought you? Why are you here? Who did they say they are? Tell me this for a fact—I need to know—is this your first time here? Or are you a friend of a father long dead, a guest from the old days? Once, crowds of other men would come to our house on visits, registering views and analyzing data, forming maps of heated interest, never too exact, registering miles away where the server has been rerouted, vessels, systems of operations, trends and loyalty, all goals benchmarked. END

C:\>

C:\> 1.exe -diagnostic

This whole story is a lie. All numbers have been masked, no ringback, all digits restricted or re-routed through somewhere that may or may not exist. Listen to those who prophesize before you, the one who does not know the flights of birds; I will not be gone long from where I love and I am never at a loss. I will return to burn where I love and all of my losses, the laying of hands and the laying of hands, the promises of a blood wedding. Find me regardless.

REFRIDGERATOR

| COREY ZELLER

They say a Chinese boy was stuffed into a small refrigerator in the kitchen of Shen Li's Fortune Moon Restaurant because he saw something the owners didn't want him to see. They stuffed him in it and played cards. They played with the sharp, quick elliptic of their shouting and smoke and the clucking of caged chickens and with the cook chopping vegetables among steaming pots and frying pans and chairs scuffing the kitchen floor and American money tossed all over and a colored, joker card pinned against the forehead of one mobster laughing some oddly high-pitched laughing and banging inside the refrigerator, banging and banging, and a woman cook coming in to help prepare drinks for the mobsters saying "what's that banging" to the other cook in Chinese and him saying "they put the boy in the refrigerator" to her and she feels her stomach drop out. She feels her stomach drop out because she knows the boy is blind so he couldn't have seen anything at all but if she says anything at all they might stuff her in the refrigerator too. BANG, BANG. And she's pouring drinks into lime-colored cups with cherry blossom trees hand-painted on them and she looks at the clock on the wall yellowed with years of cigarette smoke and cooking and god knows what else. She looks at the walls thinking about the boy in the refrigerator and how the bumps of paint on the walls look like faces. Like faces trapped permanently in the purgatory of white walls and how one afternoon she washed dishes alone and thought that the bumps of paint were really the faces of her ancestors watching her and encouraging her and telling her not to give up and throw herself off the bridge she walks over every night on her way home from work carrying brown bags of food to stuff her face with in her one-room apartment where she has nothing on the walls but a David Bowie poster even though she's never even heard a song by David Bowie in her life. Even though her husband, still in China, would beat her for having a David Bowie poster which is probably the only reason she has a David Bowie poster at all. Why live in America if you're not doing something your husband would beat you for?

And that's how it always goes for her in America. Like just before she got to work. She's sitting down unwrapping a sandwich she got from a vending machine at a shop by the bus stop. The bus that takes her to the other side of town where she still has to walk ten or twelve blocks to get to Fortune Moon. A chicken sandwich. She's sitting down to eat it and while she's eating it she sees some kind of red tendon thing sticking out of the meat and she's trying her best to pick it out. She's trying her best but it's hard to pick it out and now her fingers have been digging too deep into the chicken and it makes her sick enough to throw it away. So she throws it away and also throws away the clear wrapping and the little, plastic tray the sandwich was in. And now she's thinking of the people whose whole job it is to make little, plastic trays. And then she's thinking of the people whose job it is to make the wrapping to cover the trays in. And then the people who inscribe the tiny, nutritional facts on the wrapping. And then the people who make the ink that the other people who write the nutritional facts on use. And that's how it goes for her. She's always hungry and sick at the same time here. She sees the thread of tiny things becoming bigger things. Big like the big women she has to ride the bus with every day. The ones who don't think she speaks English. Who call her Lucy Liu.

Big. All the big, cursive lettering on their glittery shirts. Complaining about the Spanish guy hosing off the sidewalk. "Motherfucker," they say. "These are new Jordans." "Jordan." "He played basketball." "You know what basketball is?" "You speak English? "El Jordon-o play-o basketball-o, motherfucker." And they stay that way the whole ride. Complaining. Their bellies hanging out of the tops of their too-tight jeans. The varying colors of their same-style sneakers. The black alphabets of names tattooed on their necks. Complaining. About men lost. About children crying. And then they get this look in their eye. They'll be giggling and laughing and arguing with the bus driver and dancing in the aisle singing some new song on the radio like they do every day and then they'll remember that she's sitting on the back of the bus. "Lucy," they yell at her in the back of the bus. "Lucy, you better be bringing us some sweet and sour chicken tomorrow." And she looks up at them and smiles. "Yes," she says back at them and that gets them laughing. "Yes, yes, yes," they say. Squinting their eyes. Hysterical. "Yes, yes, yes."

And she sits there staring out the bus window at the coke factory sputtering into a dark cloud of ashy smoke that's been hanging in the horizon for days now. They'd been talking about it on TV. How they didn't know what contaminants were in the cloud and the mayor and other people were threatening to close it down. America. She thinks of what her father would say about her living here when she pulls out the photographs she'd taken of herself at a photo booth in the mall. How each of the four pictures were the same. Exactly the same. And not once did she smile. Even with the electronic voice inside the machine telling her to get ready for the picture. She just sat there staring at the dot on the other side of the booth. Just sat there looking at the dot long after the booth was done taking pictures of her. And it seems to her now that she's always like that. Exactly how the dead look in old photographs. How their expressions seem to know everything and nothing at all.

And when she gets off the bus her face hatchets the wind. She walks and walks feeling as if the trees are burning behind her. Incinerating. She walks and is tangled by the invisible ropes and masts of air. She feels floating. Feels jolted. Like a Chinese, Wonder Woman in her translucent jet. Fondling the see-through gears and buttons of her air ship. Like routes only the blind boy from work knows. The shortcuts he traces by memory. By hand. And she's walking. Past houses where TV is the only window. Past an empty factory whose thousand some windows hold the whole orange weight of the setting sun. This long-hand of light. How it seems to write the world slower at the end of day. Branches charred against the empty sky. With the algorithm of the sidewalks. With the cracks in their pattern. The sudden and quickly recovered trip over uneven concrete. Hiccups of graffiti. Old wrappers cutting themselves out of the earth like wildflowers below the broken eggshells of clouds. Clouds like old newspaper bunched into balls for a fire. Clouds and air. That walkie-talkie buzz of air obsessed with its own voice. The kneeling of stoops and lights. How glass seems to vanish with the clarity of nightfall. And the world turns oil-colored and in-between. Turns illegitimate and cardboard tasting. Turns like the red valentines of leaves in the broken wineglass wind. Turns marginalized. And she's walking. Past an old fountain that's covered in clear plastic. Past the trailer park that's below the red-blue roller-coaster all the kids in town ride all summer long. Past chain restaurants with the space capsule of her heart floating far past the strain of gravity and into the frostbite colors of beyond. Past beyond. Because she's always sick and hungry here. Always walking. Always walking with the percolating rhythm of the red-blue-plumed city. The flags hanging from doorways like pelts. Like old curses. Like lecturing parents who never let their pointed fingers fall down. Like a lone glacier floating further and further and further out into water and melting and melting and melting. Like her. Walking. How she's suddenly wet. Melting. Wet thinking of the black man she saw playing classical music for a dozen or so elderly people outside the library one afternoon. His broad shoulders. His hands. A song she couldn't recognize. How it made her imagine him grabbing her by the shoulders. Pushing her against the wall. With all those people on the computers inside the library. Asking questions. The way people used to trust each other. Trusting now in their favorite companion. Their electric talisman. How she still remembers the first computer she ever saw. How she had to wait for images. They'd start at the bottom or in the middle. They'd start and you'd have to wait. An image came feet-first. Waiting and modem sounds. And she's waiting for an image now. An answer. She's waiting and wishing she had a cell phone. Wishing she had a cell phone so she could pretend to talk on it. Pretend to talk on it the way the white girls do when they're alone. When they're avoiding someone. Because no one, no one, no one can see her desire. Because she's walking. She's climate-controlled. Automatic. With the crass sting of sweat in her eyes. With her memories like old, blue tins an old woman keeps her knickknacks in. Knickknacks made in China. Tins made in China. Everything made in China. America made in China. America, land of Chinese knickknacks. Land of the many hours she spent alone in her room crossing and uncrossing her legs. Crossing and uncrossing. And now she's walking into Shen Li's

Fortune Moon. She's putting her coat on the rack and getting ready for them. Their hands. How they bark "whore" at her in Chinese. And she's walking to the kitchen and says "what's that banging" to the other cook. He tells her it's the boy. The boy is locked in the fridge. And a word forms. A word forms inside her like a bright, pink scar while she pours their drinks. And she's turning to them now. And she's ready. She's stopped walking. Stopped moving.

She stops.

A SELECTION FROM "THE DAYDREAM SOCIETY"
| EVAN RETZER

I have developed a habit recently of making art out of clippings from the newspaper obituaries. I slice single words out from their surrounding bodies, deprive them of context, and then rearrange these amputations into some kind of poetic verse. Sometimes I arrange them on the wood floor of my apartment in a spiral pattern following the order of death. I manipulate the obituaries to say: *Neural Riots Wake the Shadow of Dream Highs.* My fingers get sticky with glue and stained from the rubbed off ink.

Obituaries are strange. There's a black and white photograph of the deceased—it's before they disappeared, no longer really a picture of *them;* it's a delineation of a structure their cells once formed, mapped out by a genetic predisposition. A structure once rocked by the persistent life energy that had propelled them into motion, propelled them to wake in the morning, rub their sore back, and begin their day. The body is no longer relevant to the deceased. That bird has flown.

The picture itself is a kind of motion capture of the life in memorial. A still shot clipped from the unlimited reel of experience. Undoubtedly the moment between the flash and photo capture could never accurately portray the totality of the existence of a being; and yet, we like to pretend. If we were geared to perceive our everyday experiences in the vein of obituaries, our memories would jump like stop motion video. From one to the next; the space in between—void of form or definition—is something we can't allow ourselves to recognize.

The written obit, encapsulating and reposed below the mug shot, remains at a comfortable distance from any emotional judgments. *Cyndi Blue passed away on November 7th. She was survived by her mother Dory Blue, and half-brother, Lou Fitzgerald. She spent most of her life in the city of New Orleans, where she may have been an artist, although we're not sure—since Art is essentially subjective. Friends and relatives are invited to attend the funeral mass.* This predilection towards stating only objective facts underscores a tacit, although shy, admission of the complexities of perception: no two people think exactly alike. While we'd like to say we do, while aging hippies rave on about the universal mind and psychonauts rock on their heels in dank basement apartments whispering that they can read our thoughts, the truth of it remains—when we gaze too long into the sun, each of us sees different colors.

I drop the scissors and let the obituary clippings blow restlessly across my floor, because I have to meet Marcel at a coffee shop.

∞

Marcel is scratching at his rusted brown hair ambivalently. He's got that expression on his face again; one eyeball vaguely strays from the other, off and to the left. I catch myself musing if Marcel's straying eye is searching for some kind of dysfunction in the left hemisphere of his brain, a crucial break in the logical faculty, searching for some answer he can't explain. Satsuma is busy; people crowd around each other on the pock marked patio chairs, clutching porcelain plates of runny eggs and sausage, wilted shoots of cilantro. Forks clink on these plates dispassionately, coffee mugs seem to collapse under the shade of magnolia branches like monuments to an outdated god. The rotting wooden fence around the patio gives a sparse sanctuary from the harsher concrete of the uneven street outside. Marcel and I are hunched over café au lait in a corner of the place.

"How's the apartment working out?" I ask him. He's been leasing the apartment below mine for three months now—a solid wooden affair sharing a wall with the stucco pawn shop on the first floor.

When Marcel is painting, he is the epitome of Zen. His frenetic otherworldliness cusses itself out onto canvas, releasing something in order to balance itself; nerves and ideas calm themselves over time and paint strokes. During these moments, it would not shock me to watch him tear his eyeball out and superglue it to the blank page. He etches at the blood with a bent fingernail, scraping it into some semblance of a conclusion. Marcel falls apart all over canvas—

"It's odd," he remarks. An awkward pause, and I can hear his breath quicken—"I was lying in bed last night, trying to crash out—" He stops again. "Aww, I don't know..."

"Come on," I yawn, sipping the hot coffee. From across the fence we can hear a grifter mumbling something at a passerby, a jagged, comfortable rhythm.

"So, I'm in my room, trying to sleep—and I hear a fucking voice screaming across the house—did you hear it? Around one maybe?"

I can't say that I noticed anything.

"Yes," Marcel insists, giving a deadpan look. "It's fairly insidious."

He obviously believes his story. Maybe the paint fumes have got to his head—

"What is this voice screaming about?" I ask.

At this Marcel's eyes grow downcast. "I'm not sure... something about *time*."

"Time? What exactly, about time?"

"I don't know. It's confusing—"

I can see that Marcel isn't about to open up about the specifics, so I ask him if it wasn't maybe a neighbor or domestic disturbance which he has misinterpreted the importance of.

No, Marcel insists. The voice was yelling at him and him alone. The voice was trying to communicate something to him.

"I think," muses the painter, "there is something seriously wrong with the world."

I don't know what to say to something like this.

The coffee shop door swings shut behind me with an elaborate thump. My copy of *The Daydream Society* feels jagged in my back pocket; not yet worn enough to carry comfortably. The air on the street is muggy, but there's a slight breeze; the sun beats down, drying up grass as it tries to make something of itself in sliver cracks of sidewalk. People shrink against the brick walls under awnings. My shoes *slap slap* as I walk. Ahead of me on the street stumbles what looks to be a derelict homeless, decorated in a patchwork jacket and what must once have been Sunday best pinstriped pants. As I pass closer to him, he seems to stare me down from underneath the brim of a floppy hat that has long ago lost its shape—I see a small visible area of face, covered by tangled hair. His clothes and backpack seem dusted in dried river mud. I catch myself contemplating the worn threads of the hobo's attire for a second too long, when a woman—walking faster than myself—passes me on my left. She's wearing business attire—a button shirt and black dress ensemble. Her gaze is planted fixedly ahead—and she's on a straight collision course with the shabby bum. What happens next grabs me by the lungs—my guts clench. Stepping lightly to avoid an uneven break in the sidewalk, the woman collides with the bum and passes right through him. As this is happening, I see the bum shudder—a violent spasm that shakes him from his arm down to his toes—his rat's nest of a beard shakes with the rest of him—

After a second the bum quiets down. I am caught standing on the sun scorched sidewalk with a kind of dead stare. Recognition passes silently there between the two of us; the recognition of humanity, the compassion shared by beggars and saints. I feel my breaths like quiet whispers and am sure the bum can hear them. I can see for a moment, in the shade under his hat, almost pupil-less eyes, pulsing black—in a chaos of now, I see him beginning to steal towards me, shuffling with slow, painful steps. I startle out of this reverie and step aside, off the sidewalk; the figure shuffles past me—I can hear the audible ticking of a pocket watch—all recognition lost, his attention cast ahead of him; he passes me, forgotten. When I turn around, instinctively, to see where he was going, he is gone. In a state of confusion, I run to the alley that traces out the back patio of Satsuma looking for him. No, he is gone.

Sun-induced hallucinations are a bitch.

SELECTIONS FROM THE 2016 CATALOGUE

POEM FROM IRFAN ABRAHIM'S LAST BOOK
| JUSTIN SIROIS

before we went to bed last night, I said to my wife
tomorrow, all day, only lie to me—tell me nothing true and
I will listen to your weird lies and I won't judge a
single word

she shook her head like a wind strangled tree
  sure, whatever. Why did I marry a poet?

moonlight. Goat bells and motor bikes outside our window—the breeze
doesn't lie when her bare shoulders change the tempo of its whisper
I watch her sleep and feel like a teenager again

in the morning, I asked her where she put my shoes
  on the roof, up high, don't be stupid

and I asked what she was making for breakfast
  sunglasses with honey and dates, milk too

really? I asked

  do you want Ray-Ban of Oakley?

whatever you're having! I called from the living room,
barefoot, I walked outside to scan the roof for my shoes

                              *

I love this life we live in the city
Baghdad—a book inside every brick—this secret isn't a

secret at all

from outside, I watch my wife frying eggs
no one can take me from her. No one can take her from me

I tap on the window

My wife's weird lies continued through lunch and the afternoon—she said she wanted the couch moved into the upstairs bathroom

    It'll fit. I measured the damn thing three times

from the living room, I dragged the couch to the foot of the stairs, snagging electric cords and lamps, and I laid on it and sipped tea while the sunlight did that thing to the room that we love so much. To a fault, the sun never told a lie. It will fire with integrity until it dies and we die with it. Allah created tea leaves and tea leaves created conversation and there is no lie in that. Men talk like their fathers. Women talk like the future. Between sexes—I am neither and both—the Disaster poet

    how does it look?
what?
    the couch? In the bathroom?

I knew not to answer. The couch is the most honest piece of furniture in the house. I pry the cushions apart, smelling the crumby tomb, and whisper all the things I want to happen this year—we'll find the money for a new roof, my wife will stop lying to me, my daughter will make the soccer team, I will finish this poem

    Well?

In this land, nothing is unintentional. Man invented the accident and the mistake. In this land, a couch can be a sarcophagus for a family

she comes and kisses me

Well?

In the evening, I take a walk and watch my daughter
from afar—how every gesture she makes with her friends
is honest music—how I wish I could move like that again

She kicks but misses the goal. I know not to wave. Here
is the grain of sand I've been carrying all my life, it swirls in my heart,
worms through my veins like a misbehaving atom. Sprinkle it over
my grave. My wife texts

We need bread. Can you pick some up?

I wonder if she's lying. I sneak a cigarette, taste the imported soil and
sun with each burn. Walk to Al Mutanabbi Street, through the grids of
books and bad teeth, where I become that same grain of sand circulating
through the heart of the city—just one voice
in the endless bombardment

Hello. I am honored to be here. Among you prophets. Among you read-
ers. Hello. I am honored to be here. Sipping more tea. Giving a friend a
smoke. Hello. I am honored to be here. Among you young soldiers. With
the same sweat. The same mouth. The same wonder. Hello. I am

honored

Well?

A POEM FROM *"CAREFUL MOUNTAIN"*
| *SARA JUNE WOODS*

Dear Juniper,

It was great to hear from you again.
We see each other all the time, I know,
but it's always like someone handed me
a freshly cut watermelon I wasn't expecting.
You are beautiful, & I am a girl with a name
like a state park, or I aspire to be nearer
to that at some point before the rain comes.

What are your arms doing right now?
Are you holding them like this, like I am
holding mine right now, like I held them
on the day we came home & the whole
apartment was filled wall-to-wall with pink
balloons & we just popped our way to bed?
Remember how we didn't even bother
with the other ones, how we were so tired,
& so we slept for a few lifetimes & woke
up as presidents? I was the president of
smoking or some other thing I don't really do
anymore & you were the president of the tiny
lizards we used to find out crawling by the dumpster.

Is there something spiritual in making
more intentional fashion decisions
or am I making this up?
I mean I am making this up
but am I right?

I mean if I told you I was
a dragon or a cloud full
of birds you can't see
or a bear in a forest
who just ate the whole forest
but regrets it, would you believe me
or would the whole world I've got,
or at least the parts I trust carefully,
come down crushing like the weak
ceiling above your friend's
friend's bassinet?

The thread my house is hanging by
could pop any second & bring this whole
taco joint with it & you & everyone
are all made of scissors lately.
When did that happen?
When did crying all the time get so dang cool?
When did this parking lot fill up with cars
that are about things? Was I not paying attention?
Because this car is about dying &
that car is about what people say
to themselves in the shower &
that car is about how much I love
you when your hair is wet.

Your friend talks too rough sometimes
& I'm a photograph of the sound you just
made when I told you about dogs driving but
I still have to haul this suitcase full of water
to a new location. People like drugs
because they're the closest
to magic but real magic exists it just
doesn't care about what we want,
& I don't blame it. I'm just a parked car somewhere.
I'm just one of these closets in a room full
of closets but I'm all painted shut

so just trust me when I say there's
a whole lot of nice ponies hanging
out even if you can't get to them
to scruffle their ears.

We don't think the sun is too strong
in wintertime but it's just far away
& that's how I feel right now,
like I'm driving this truck with
broom handles connected to
broom handles & I'm out
sitting on the tailgate, trying
to keep my hair in place.
I just want to see what happens
when it finds its own length.

GROWING UP
| CTCH BSNSS

you pretend you're you again

when you look over the sink

seeing someone who might be

a neighbor or a myopic trope

others were quickly abandoned

to begin with they were drugs

only older than us

i wish that was all i'd said

until there you were in kind

gripping parted palms swiftly

trading places instead of

watching tv in ac homes

FOR SHAME

| ANDREW MILLER

Sentimentality seems like a desperate last grasp at redemption before committing the emotional suicide of self-examination on the page; but shame has a way of rewriting beginnings, endings, and everything else sometimes. I'm not entirely sure that what you are reading is my creation as definition of self, or if the words have spilled across these pages in a revolt against my right brain - instead defining me more truthfully than my more pragmatic side would ever allow.

I believe that this is a revolt.

I believe that words are not just symbols.

I believe that words make things real.

During the final day of my father's life we had that cliché ending, the one where with his last bit of strength he told me he loves me. It was the first time his voice sounded weak to me, on this last day of his life, in what would be some of his final words.

"I love you," barely audible and followed with a wheeze and a cough and a gentle squeeze of my hand. He passed away before the sun rose the next day, speaking only a few more words to my mother before he was dead.

I'm so glad my mom got his last words, I'm so glad he gave those to her. I was only in that room for my mom initially, and so I'm still years later trying to understand what he meant by telling me he loved me. I'm still trying to believe that his words made that love real. And I'm so glad my mom got his last words that early morning before he died, because I'm certain I didn't deserve that final gift.

Dad was in hospice, dying of complications related to lymphoma and lupus; my mom had let my sister and I know only hours earlier that if we were coming, we'd better come now. I would make the 6 hour drive in less than 5 hours, borrowing my girlfriend's car and dragging her along because my only other option was an unreliable motorbike. On the drive

I would consider the number of death's my family had suffered over that previous year. I would be thankful for the past year or so of sobriety I had managed to string together after another disastrous relationship crumbled. I would fight with my daughter's mother over how to get my daughter there to Michigan, to let her be a part of her grandfather's funeral. I would sign my final divorce papers only a couple weeks after this day. I would read a eulogy that I had written for my father, unsure that anything I was saying was true. I would feel ashamed of the history of my life and of my history with my father as I stared blankly out over a church full of mourners, who would later recall what a great friend, teacher and coach he had been to them.

Shame is a powerful weapon.

I embrace shame like a scalpel.

I embrace shame like a scalpel and eviscerate my ego and empty myself of any concept of who I am, who I was; filling the void with self-deprecation.

Immanuel Kant argued that freedom and morality are directly linked, and in opposition to shame. For Kant, only if you have the freedom to choose to do the right thing, the moral thing, the thing that every single human is capable of, can you then be moral. However, acting on shame means being shackled to motives that are not free, that can never be moral.

Reacting to the shame, filled with such guilt, I wonder if I'll ever be free.

That night of death

That night moon bright

Reflecting the sun's melting starlight

A frozen Lake Mack, a dammed spring awaiting the moment tide sets it free

Corrupting barriers, a trickle, a stream, carrying foreign seed and soil

Deep history worn into shallow pebbles, deposited on new shores

Life begetting life, the journey of generations

Sequence of exponential numbers unable, unwilling to deviate from the pattern

Begins with one, then two, then broadens as it uncoils

I'm filled with such guilt, such shame

I'm unwilling to deviate from the pattern

I wonder if I'll ever be moral

I wonder if I'll ever be free

I wonder if I'll ever be free
If I'll ever be free.

A SELECTION FROM "AMERICAN MARY"
| ALEXANDRA NAUGHTON

Sunken islands. We are living on sunken islands.

Well, they feel sunken, like hungover eyes all peeping only slightly because it's straining. Like there isn't much space to move around in. Like the way you act when we're in public together.

There is no green anything. I can see the Statue of Liberty from my Philly window, Manhattan's metallic cones hundreds of stories high like quills jutting, a beastly back and head submerged like it can't deal anymore, smack needles in sidewalk cracks. I guess I always wanted to live in the big city.

All those offices. Fuck.

It's coming soon I think, and I touch that part of my back that doesn't touch the bed. It's like a pocket. It's a space for my hand. I touch that part of my back just above my ass and feel knuckles against spine. Everyone is looking for security.

I know or I don't. I leave.

I walk outside and join melting faces beginning a crowded commute. I don't think I've ever been good at any of my jobs. I used to think it was because I've never been paid enough to give a shit but lately I've been feeling like that wouldn't change anything. I don't know how some people do it. How can I perform for another first.

We take a deep breath, scrape our feet, and step inside a bus with no roof, just poles to grasp. Better for everyone, emissions, they say, but really the city is strapped. At least for us. We can complain and we do, it's like a song. We all know the words and the right time to sing it. Right after exchanging pleasantries.

Old ladies carry shopping bags stuffed with recycling. They mostly crouch or prop themselves on the accordion panels but one standing slips and reaches out to hold my leg for stability. Almost a daily occurrence. I look down and we smile at each other.

You can get used to anything if you don't care about anything.

Watching pink and orange clouds through an opening. They don't float or drift, they wallow and stay with you, less like puffs or wisps and more like a neon mashed potato spread, falling heavy and clumping.

Every day is an experiment in distractions. I can't concentrate on anything outside for too long, it just makes me remember. I try singing songs that I like in my head for comfort and familiarity. Passing where the Schuylkill was, now just a curdled puddle.

Something like a cavity, like sticking a soft spot.

From Strawberry Mansion Bridge dots wade. People with plastic up to ankles collect cans. Trash is burning, their choking fumes enrobe. The lady curled around my calf rummages through bags for a sheet of newspaper to cover her face.

Outside the still open South street occult shop, patrons wait to grab the last of the bat's blood. We write our regrets in letters.

We always write letters, it's the only place we know how to hide.

WHY I WAS NOT IN NEW JERSEY FOR CHRISTMAS IN 1997

| TOBIAS CARROLL

If I'm going to be honest, I should probably say that things in my life went awry starting in the second half of 1997. Nothing tragic was involved, but I felt out of my depth, wrestling with a kind of sustained failure that stretched over weeks and months, sometimes receding before just as quickly leaping back into place. I was halfway through college, interning at a film's production office in Soho. Sometimes I'd get drafted to come in on weekends to sign for FedEx deliveries. I'd sit and read Hubert Selby Jr. and wonder if I should stop being straight edge.

The job wrapped up in the third week of December. I was pretty much done with finals by the time I received an email telling me to come down and pick up a crew jacket. This was pretty convenient: the office was south of my dorm, and south of there was a friend's apartment near the Seaport, where I had to drop off a book that I'd been lent. I had a ten-minute walk to get to the office and I figured, why wear a jacket when I'd be getting one when I arrived? And so I was brisk in my walking–so brisk, in fact, that I began sweating. Sweating without a jacket in forty-degree weather; I probably should have gleaned that something was wrong. And then I was in the jacket, and I felt like I was gushing. Sweat ran into my eyes, blurring contact lenses and earning me some stares as I continued on. I figured I'd flush it out of me; it made sense at the time. I got to my friend's apartment, handed off the book, got some more stares, and found my way to the subway. Hello, Broadway-Nassau. Hello, stairways up and down and unclear signage. I spent ten minutes on one platform before I realized it was the wrong one; I found my way down some more stairs, and stepped on board that train when it came. In the initial announcement, it sounded like the conductor was saying it was the E.

I was the only one on the car. I took off my jacket and folded it in my lap and felt the train move. And on we went; no stops were made for the next hour. Finally, I heard the voice of the conductor: "This is the 8 line, making express stops to Los Angeles. Next stop on this train will be Marfa, Texas. Marfa is the next stop." And I thought, fuck this year.

My fever broke somewhere under what I believe to have been Tennessee. Sometimes we would stop; the doors would open, and I would hear the conductor's voice say, "Please return to the train in an hour." And so I'd step onto these platforms under the earth and stretch my legs. There were vending machines there, and shower stalls you could rent, all automated. I'd clean up and feed myself and would get back on the train. My new jacket became my pillow soon enough; it never felt soft. I bought reading material there, most science fiction novels I'd already read in high school.

The 8 express stopped at Marfa; no one got off, and no one got on. The name of the next stop came out garbled, and it was another two days under the earth before we got there. I thought, shit, I don't know anyone in Los Angeles; why wait even longer? Four hours later, we came to the next station, the one with the indistinct name. I stepped out of the train and onto the lonesome platform and looked around. No one else was there, either on the platform or near the turnstiles I stepped through or the steps leading above ground. Here it was hot; here my sweat was sensible. There was a newsstand and a pay phone beside the desert station. I looked at the newspapers and saw that it was January, and that was when it hit me, that I was late for so many things.

SAD WOMAN
| ASHLEY FARMER

I never saw a sad woman
Buying a Chanel bag.
Diamonds are my favorite
Shape like little friends
From a different perspective.
But I know what it is
To be human:
Bathtubs and the minimum
Sunlight. Sad sad women.

YOU ARE READING THIS.

THE NEW MIDDLE CLASS
| DOLAN MORGAN

"Take your time, Amy," Dr. Kenston says, as if time were a thing to be taken. As if a doctor could forget that it's time that does the taking.

"Breathe," he says, and I do. We all do. Michael, me, everyone in the world. We all follow this doctor's advice for a while. Of course. But then.

Christ, Michael.

Michael is calm, somehow. I can't understand it. He sits in his wooden armchair, here at the large desk, in this awful hospital, and smiles. Like he is faced not with mortality but merely a pointless decision between shades of paint. Pleasant tones, clever names. Muted greens. Shallow blues and slate. How does he still have access to such ease and serenity, I wonder. Is there a secret pool of knowledge into which illness finally let's us drift? Trade good health for a single, pure fact about the world. Something otherwise hidden that might, in its revelation, bestow upon Michael great calm. Maybe he has this knowledge but cannot share it with anyone, not even me. How painful that would be for him, I think, to keep that secret. "Just take your time, Amy," Dr. Kenston says again. Why is it so much easier for me to indulge in imaginary burdens than to actually face the ones right here in front of me. Muted greens. Shallow blues and slate. Either way, Michael is utter calm, just air, just nothing, and I'm jittering, anxious, unfolding like some failed paper plane, even though it's Michael that's dying, even though it's Michael that time is taking.

"Amy," he says, "I'm ready whenever you are. We can do this." I am thirty years old. He puts his hand on mine in the office in the hospital in the city where we live. He is almost thirty-two. I'm not ready. I'll never be ready.

"I'm ready," I say.

Dr. Kenston nods, rotates his chair closer to Michael's, plants his feet on the pink tile and adjusts a white coat. "This will only take a moment, it's very brief," he says, all empathy and comfort. He rolls up Michael's sleeve, administers a small injection, then asks Michael to recline his chair and unbutton his shirt. Dr. Kenston rubs an acrid solution over Michael's bare belly. "You'll feel a bit of pressure," he says, revealing a knife.

Dr. Kenston makes an incision in Michael's abdomen, maybe four inches long on the right-hand side, and then swabs away the blood. There is a lot. He massages the flesh around the opening with his large hands, first in broad waves and then in tight circles. Michael smiles at me, nods, always an anchor. The doctor leans in close to the wound, as if to smell or taste it, and begins to whisper. I cannot hear what he says.

"Take your time," I imagine, or "breathe."

Then the skin spreads apart, as if on its own, and the Replacement flowers out. Its brown, rippling head slips from the wound, then more of it. White layers of fat gleam where the cut has stretched tight.

I see the serenity fade from Michael's face. Whatever pure truth had been granted him by illness, it is gone now.

The Replacement is at once like a large tongue and a hard, knotted root. A wet winter branch teasing through a hole in the fence. It projects from Michael's side, half in half out, and turns toward the light.

The Replacement stretches as if yawning, then gurgles out a mix of mucus, bile, and blood from what must be a kind of nascent mouth.

"Hello," the doctor says to the Replacement. "I'd like to introduce you to someone. Her name is Amy."

"Hello, Amy," the Replacement coughs.

*

Over the next few months, I accompany Michael three times a week to sessions intended to better acquaint me with his Replacement.

At first, Dr. Kenston needs to remake the incision at the start of every meeting so that we can commence our smalltalk, icebreakers, and goal setting. This is how we begin to know each other. The doctor cuts Michael open, leads us through a series of interpersonal sharing games (quizzes, confessions, trust falls), and then packs the Replacement back into its hole. It's clean and easy. I talk about my childhood. The Replacement asks questions about what it means to be alive. Michael tries to transfer his anxiety about death into joy for the Replacement's burgeoning new life. "It's really exciting," Michael says, clenching his fist. When we leave, I can almost pretend it isn't real.

The doctor's incisions quickly become unnecessary, though, because the Replacement stops retreating into Michael's body at the close of sessions. Too big. It simply remains dangling from his side at all times.

On the car ride home. At work. In bed. The bathroom. Everywhere. There is no getting away from it.

Michael struggles with this sudden loss of privacy. It's too much for him, and he wants to discuss it at the next meeting.

"I don't have time to myself, either, you know," the Replacement says bitterly.

Michael starts to interrupt, but Dr. Kenston reminds him that the Replacement has the talking stick right now. "You've lived a whole life on your own, Michael," it says. "I've never had that. I've never been by myself. Never even existed completely outside of your abdomen."

I consider the moments in my life that I've been truly alone, versus the times I've been irretrievably wrapped up in the body and life of another. I can't remember when I stopped being shocked at their inevitable intersection.

With Dr. Kenston's help, we reach a sort of compromise. When Michael needs time to himself, the Replacement will wear a small hoodie and submit to swaddling.

At home, we give it a try. "I'm glad we talked this out," the Replacement says and wiggles into his little sock. It's new and gleaming. Then Michael pulls him against his chest and stretches the swaddling scarf around them both.

It looks ridiculous but kind of works, so Michael and I kind of have sex. It's sloppy, rehearsed and almost depressing, and in some ways doesn't so much happen as pretend to happen, but it's better than nothing I think.

In this way, life is somewhat normal for a time.

But the Replacement is not satisfied. He also wants to be by himself. Dr. Kenston says that's his right, of course. Apparently, there's a hood for that too.

At home, we give it a try.

I drag the large cloth bag over Michael's head, then pull it down to his feet and help the Replacement poke through the pre-made hole. I guide Michael to the floor, where he stretches out by the coffee table, and I cover him with the additional solitude blankets. He shuffles a bit, then goes still.

The Replacement looks like a potted plant left atop unwashed clothes. Michael doesn't look like anything at all. Like nothing.

"Why are you crying?" the Replacement asks.

I lie down next to the pile of blankets and rub my hand along its soft fabric.

"This is my time to be alone," the Replacement says. "Aren't you going to leave?"

I can hear Michael breathing, can feel the warmth of his body, but I can't see him. I can only imagine him. When I was a child, I would crawl out of bed and press my face to the floor like this. I would rub the carpet on my cheeks and try to picture the whole universe. The ocean, other planets. Michael shifts a bit. I close my eyes and pull tufts of blanket tight into my hands. I can't squeeze hard enough.

"You know what's funny?" the Replacement says. "Soon it will be Michael that dangles from my body."

Muted greens. Shallow blues and slate.

*

When Michael becomes paralyzed and unable to speak later that summer, the Replacement has already completed his physical therapy sessions, through which he has grown in strength and size, learning to walk and wear Michael's clothes.

The Replacement begins attending professional development workshops to smooth his transition into Michael's old job at the university. As is customary, the Replacement adopts the name "Michael".

Michael lives with me in our home. Michael needs to be fed and washed. Michael eats dinner with me and helps clean around the house. Michael sees and acknowledges my presence, I think, and he knows that I am here. Michael learns to ride a bike, order takeout. Michael dangles helplessly from Michael's body, like toilet paper from the bottom of a shoe.

Dr. Kenston says it's clichéd to compare our situation to Invasion of the Body Snatchers, but I don't care what's clichéd and what isn't if it hurts this much.

He says my line of thinking is akin to a fear of vaccinations: ill-conceived and misinformed, lacking all footholds in medical science. But even I know that grief exists beyond the reach of facts.

He says stop interrupting, that he has the talking stick, that I need to internalize the idea that cancer cannot be cured, that we can only manage and learn to live with it, that allowing our ailments to evolve into productive members of society is maybe even better than a cure. Symbiosis. I feel sick.

Finally, he says, there really is an afterlife, but we don't have to wait for it. It is here with us now and it's willing to form a new, reliable labor force.

When I break the talking stick over the afterlife's knotted, wormy face, Dr. Kenston refers our case to a specialist.

Which doesn't matter, obviously, because Michael is going to die. We all know that now. And, no, I don't mean Michael. I mean Michael. He has to die.

I stare into his drooping eyes, hoping he understands just how much I know this, and with what certainty.

*

Autumn comes, and with it sweaters, scarves, and the distant smell of burning wood. Amy says that my affection for every saccharine trope of the season disgusts her. Oh, Amy. Still, I am happy to be wrapped up in all this warm cloth. It takes me back, back before the funeral, back when I lived inside a man.

And the flavors! I can hardly contain myself with the flavors.

I am waiting in line at the cafe for a Pumpkin Spice Latte, and probably I will die from too much joy. I am thinking about warm cinnamon and crunchy leaves and pie when I notice my server is a replacement, too, fully grown. This discovery isn't unusual by itself (replacements work in every branch of industry), but by sheer coincidence, this one happens to be named Michael. That's my name! I can hardly believe it.

He's awkward, stumbling through the motions, but here and working, which is admirable. Good for him.

I think of the life out of which he must have grown. Somewhere, another Michael, one I've never met or known, withered in front of his family, which is hard, and out of that failing body emerged this earnest barista, which is hopeful.

Yes. He gives us all hope, I say to myself, as the barista fumbles with change and gets flustered at the register, saying "I'm sorry, I'm sorry" and crying into his twisted hands.

A wet winter branch teasing through a hole in the fence, Amy always says. About me. Which I've never really understood before now.

He so obviously does not belong here. I mean, nobody belongs here, really, and we're all just lucky to have this rare opportunity despite the odds, I know I know, but I hope I'm luckier than this poor idiot.

At home, Amy is cutting vegetables. Well, not really. She's standing over the sink with a large knife in her hand, a pepper on the counter. "Don't fucking talk to me," she says, "don't even look at me." It's a thing we do from time to time. You know. Or: it's a thing we do, minus the knife. The knife is new. Amy stares at it like it's the first time she's ever seen it.

Anyway, I know my cue. Gotta give Amy her space.

In the living room, I drag the large cloth bag over my head, then pull it down to my feet. I get on the ground. Through the little hole, I pull over the extra solitude blankets. I stay perfectly still and don't make a sound. Just the way she likes it.

Then I hear a rustling along the carpet, feel something press along my back.

I can hear Amy breathing. I can feel the warmth of her body, but I can't see her. I can only imagine her. I close my eyes. I feel my cheeks. The ocean, other planets. Muted greens. Shallow blues and slate.

I hear Amy say my name and feel an ache I don't understand. There's something I need to ask her soon. I really want to know. On certain days, how can you tell the difference between Autumn and Spring?

THERE IS NO SUCH THING AS APOLITICAL ART DUMB ASS

| JOSHUA JENNIFER ESPINOZA

first there was nothing
then god created a man & immediately she said
"i've made a huge mistake"
it's okay god
i make mistakes all the time
like believing in people
like questioning myself
like my shaking hands gripping empty air
while i try to say what i believe loudly
there is a silence in me that is not deep
it does not go on forever
it is only a pause
a hesitation
the thing you lack in your fingers
as you tell me about beauty
"beauty is the absence of meaning"
some asshole once said
but the only thing i do for its own sake
is continue not to die
every morning i wake up & avoid the mirror
as i read the buried headlines
about buried trans women
beauty doesn't exist
words are bullshit
there is only the anger that keeps you going
out the front door into a world full of knives
there is only the fear you have
of living something like a life

i've lived several lives
subsisting on spite & fuck its
the only aesthetic i have left is survival
so if you want to see something truly beautiful
stop killing us
& then stare at the sky & shut the fuck up forever

MOMENTS FROM HIGH SCHOOL
| MADISON LANGSTON

got really high and went to the mall and thought everyone in the food court was a cop

took ecstasy before senior homecoming dance, arrived at dance to find dad was the dj

vague memory of driving home very slowly through (possibly hallucinted) road work while extremely high on ether

fell asleep in cheerleading coach's classroom instead of going to lunch, got suspended for skipping class

stood in friends parents yard with two of my friends, one friend got on all fours behind me and the other friend pushed me causing me to fall over friend on all fours, felt really scared

went to mexican restaurant with ~5 other girls after we participated in a beauty walk

vague memory of getting in trouble/getting 'called out' for yawning at ~7am during cheerleading camp

did coke for the first time

did coke in a dippin dots bathroom

teacher 'got in my face' and asked if i was a christian, felt confused and sleepy woke up on the ground tripping on acid at a string cheese concert, chubby man in overalls happily dancing over me

3 WAYS I DON'T WANT TO DIE
| MATTHEW SIMMONS

Alan,

I've been thinking a lot about it and I've decided some things. There are some very specific ways that I don't want to die and I think that the best thing to do is for me to go ahead and enumerate them here in this letter to you because I believe that even though the universe is a dark and unjust place—the sort of place where one might find oneself on the business end of a death that one fears the most—it also has stitched into its makeup a system for prioritizing stunning novelties on those within it that are capable of that kind of thing. The universe— consciously or unconsciously, depending on your worldview—moves toward making things new and surprising. So I believe strongly that by putting these thoughts out there into the world, I am in some way inoculating myself from them. Only time will tell, I suppose.

1) I don' t want to die alone in the office while I'm sitting at my desk working and fielding texts from you about when I think I am going to maybe be home for dinner or a late dinner or a very late dinner. I don't want to be alone and in the half-dark, annoyed and trying to make sense of the schedules of the many people I support. Annoyed at my phone on my desk or in my pocket when it shudders with a text from you asking when I'm going to head home. Annoyed when it seems like you just texted me and I responded. Annoyed when I realize that it was forty minutes ago that you texted me, not five minutes ago, and it makes perfect sense you are texting me again. I don't want to die an- noyed by whatever day of the week it is, which is just like every other day of the week at my job. Which is just like the first day at my job. Which is just like, I'm betting, the last day at my job. I don't want to die annoyed because there is no emotional state of less consequence than annoyance. There is no more worthless way to feel about things

than to be annoyed by them. I don't want that to be the last way I feel. I'd prefer anger or even sadness. Confusion. Hopelessness. Anything but annoyance.

I don't want to die at 8:45pm in my cubicle after everyone else has gone home and the only sound is the sound of the guy from Operations whistling "Dust in the Wind" over and over and over again like he does. The one who whistles the first verse and then the chorus, and then repeats the chorus, and then does the verse, and then repeats the verse, and then does the chorus four or five more times. And never anything else. Just those two sections of the song, over and over. No bridge. No violin solo. I don't want to, say, have a brain aneurysm rupture while I'm listening to him do that. I don't want to die and start falling into my own consciousness and find myself trapped in some sort of dustbowl purgatory, my soul alone and haunting a vast, empty prairie, followed for all eternity by a high, lonely sound.

2) I don't want to die in a car accident, especially now that I have figured out how to put the car seat into the back. And I don't think it's ever going to come out. It took me so long to figure out how to loosen the buckle of the seatbelt and feed it around the back of the car seat's base, and strap it in tight. I don't think I can remove it. I don't want to remove it. I don't want to go through that again.

Honestly, I don't want to try. I just want it to stay in there and I don't care if that means we won't be able to have a fourth person in the car ever again. I really just don't care. I still have a bruise on the top of my hand from the evening I spent trying to get the car seat in the car. And because there isn't a baby to use the car seat yet, dying in a car accident in a car with an as-of-yet only aspirational car seat seems like one of the most intensely sad ways to die. Like one of those, "Oh, how sad. He was looking toward the future but he'll never see it come," sorts of deaths that is so popular with sentimental people. I don't want to die for the emotional catharsis of sentimental people.

I don't want to be reaching for the radio and be struck by an inattentive teenager. I don't want to feel my body in motion and have my soul push free from my body, stuck and straining until it snaps away. I don't want my soul in motion to be my eternal state, speeding away from the car forever and ever, speeding up and speeding up until I am going so fast, I'm everywhere in the universe all at once, and then I am the universe and have to feel everything that the universe feels for always, and all because someone was texting someone else that they would be there soon.

3) I don't want to die in St. Petersburg, beaten to death, standing outside an orphanage because you and I are holding hands. I have been watching all the videos on Youtube about the people in Russia who target young gay men or gay couples, and how the police don't really do much about it. And say that's what happens: we go to Russia and we find an orphanage in, I guess, St. Petersburg—you know more about this stuff than I do because you're the one looking into it—and we're nervous and excited and in order to alleviate some of the stress we are feeling, we do what we always do. We do what lots of people do. You grab my hand. You step closer and our shoulders touch. Our arms touch. Our legs touch.

Anyone seeing that would understand the gesture. Anyone seeing that would know what the relationship between us is. Everybody knows about that way that people make contact with one another in times of stress when those people are emotionally invested in one another.

What if the wrong person sees that, and that person is with other wrong people? What if we get harassed, and then we get attacked? What if, so close to what we want, we're killed? We die? What if our hands are together, and then they are ripped apart, and we spin away and spin away outward and we never see each other again? Or just experience each other again? All because we held hands?

I don't want to die like that.

Love,
Me

NIGHT OCEAN
| JANICE LEE

One must be receptive, receptive to the image at the moment it appears.
—Gaston Bachelard, *The Poetics of Space*

In one space the safety and cleanliness of a structured space, in another, the threat of extinction.

It is night, and it is dark, and always, faced with the vastness of an ocean that is black and moving and roaring, the threat of extinction, of utter annihilation. Yours. His. Everyone's.

The placid expressions of late-night joggers seem almost completely irrelevant next to that blackness that could swallow you whole. This is the closest to infinity you can get out here. Stains on the night. Surpassing.

How else can I say "I ever—"

Am I looking for death in all of these spaces?

What approaches over the water?

What the darkness conjures is an oath, the last and final breath, an expiration, that comes again and again with every roar of the tide coming in, with every absence of sight (you can't see anything in this light, it is blurry, the different darknesses run together, the horizon line a thick black border: phantom, ambiguous, wandering). The dilemma of sight requires the ghosting of memory, the water a translation of water, the darkness a distortion of ocean. What is exposed in the air? It is cold. One hardly has the opportunity to feel cold anymore.

Finding death.

Thundering sounds.

We walk slowly across the sand, light spreading.
We walk slowly across the water, light spreading.
We walk slowly across the sky, light spreading.

Can you grasp the simple feeling of empathy out here? That is, it's now impossible to feel empathy for anything. The disappearance of empathy as looming and imminent and dangerous as the catastrophic event that is yet to tear the planet apart. The planet will be torn apart. Can't you feel it coming?

The *feeling* of a ringing in my ears before an explosion, before something that is about to happen.

> Poetry is a soul inaugurating a form.
> —Pierre-Jean Jouve

What of the form if darkness? What of the form if a formless form, an ocean? What of resonance? Of temperature? Of being in love with your back against the rest of the entire planet on the other side of that blackening black under that strangely deep, profoundly blue sky. The darkest blue night.

The moon thinks it's hiding, exposed again, shifting lights.

That we can call such a breathless and formless thing a word: OCEAN. That we can hold these fixed memories of vertigo, moving lights, faces, all recalled by the sound of the water, the birds running along the shoreline, a handful of sand to feel the beach as a concrete thing. The feeling of sand is cold and expected. The feeling of loss, the breath that comes when you let the grains drop, and the arms that wrap themselves around you afterward, unexpected tremblings of moments.

I take steps towards one of the three birds. It refuses to fly, runs quickly over to the right.

So I waver towards the right, take a few steps toward another bird.

You ask me: *Why are you separating them?*

I don't know. I have no intention in mind.

In response to the perceived continuity of black ocean, I make a gesture filled with uncertainty and regret. Indeed, why?

Seek out the silence that makes your ears ring.

> At times, the simpler the image, the vaster the dream.
>
> We want to see and yet we are afraid to see. This is the perceptible threshold of all knowledge, the threshold upon which interest wavers, falters, then returns.
> —Gaston Bachelard, *The Poetics of Space*

The recognition that the end is very near. It is your responsibility. The guilt, the wound, the future.

Future wound guilt is a conjuration is a towards gesture, illegible but audible, inherited, present, the smell of archived lies and salt.

I'll come to you in the morning, the message of water.

I'll come again or I will be there already and I'll pass through each of the phantoms already circling, circling, sand and broken glass in my hand.

The ocean will speak when there is silence. There will be silence when we stop screaming. We will not stop screaming until we are all already dead.

Apocalypse no longer means the end days no longer means something to-come. It is the way of life, the expression of a permanently muted voice, the abundance of a certain quality of light, meditating under the moon, the inability to capture anything in an image.

We walk slowly across the sand, arms meeting.
We walk slowly across the sand, light meeting.
We walk slowly across the sand, hands meeting.

The gift that you can not capture the image. The memory becomes the copy becomes the whisper becomes the oath.

I am honest when I say, *I love you.*

I am honest when I say, *I am terrified.*

I am honest when I say, *I don't understand any of this. You.*

The ocean is terrifying and it may swallow me whole, drowning in water or limbs torn apart by a bracketing of excess, but I am more terrified of my love for you. I don't understand where it comes from.

Do you understand that when the answers to your questions are, *I don't know*, it's not for lack of enthusiasm or decisiveness, it is the perceived trauma of some dark light that may enter at any minute. This is my crisis, not yours. It is my issue and failure, not yours. When I say, *I love you* and *I don't know*, these statements in the same sentence, same breath, same expression of oblivion, this is the most honest I can be.

We are all fated for failure.

But that failure can be caressed with the patient strokes of the blue waves and we can hold hands under the moonlight and draw swirls in the sky with our fingers to manipulate the clouds. We can fall together, and when they finally tear me away from you, I will not scream.

PLEASE TELL ME I AM JUST KIDDING ABOUT THIS, CRUMBS FROM MY SANDWICH FALLING IN BETWEEN MY BREASTS

| LAURA MARIE MARCIANO

Some are born into money. Others work for it. I am what they call an expectation. The traffic drones, where drones is a noun. The MoMa has an excellent view of the city. The windows are perfect frames for four story delis. Know that it might be possible to fall in love with anything that gives you enough attention. "So many people are dying from tornadoes and I'm just sitting here eating potatoes." When it's hot outside skin is hot, the traffic of blood right below the surface becomes tense and bottle necks into her nipples when he says something sweet, waiting for the red school house of his mouth to alleviate suffering. If we can't save the people from natural disaster, at least we can save one another from feeling alone. My father sounds like an old man on the phone. I know this because I use to listen up to him and now I listen down. I was fifteen sitting in the back of his eggplant colored Dodge caravan when I told him that I knew I was smarter then a lot of adults. I know this because now I am an adult and no one uses cordless phones anymore at home. The scar across your nose is deep and I've seen it fill with rain water on a depressing sunday morning after the local 12 news. Imagine immersion into a swimming pool of gold coins, suffocating the flow to the nipples, creating double shadows of loneliness against prismatic hearts. I wouldn't mind wrapping my legs about your neck and then talking about failure some time after over orange berry tea. Face painted children, red, sliver war stripes running in thick green dreamlands. the playground of normalcy and the sand box of eccentricity. The hours of McDonald's happy meal toys and french fries stuck like dead ants to the floor of the car. I will conceive our first child in a gas station on a road trip to LA when I've been out of work. Your skin will be tan by then. We won't have been able to make it to the hotel. We'll name him Shell. Please tell me I am just kidding about this, crumbs from my sandwich falling in between my breasts.

HOW TO BECOME A BETTER SOCIOPATH
| CAROLYN ZAIKOWSKI

RING

You are a sociopath. Basically what this means, is that you have an inability to relate to the pain of others. Your emotional system is a different make and model than the norm and, most likely, you have never felt the thing that most people think of as empathy. Many people in civilized society consider this problematic to some degree. Terms often used interchangeably with sociopath include psychopath and antisocial personality.

In this section you will learn to associate images of muddy footprints with your sociopathic tendencies. We will begin by invoking some of your sense-memories of maiming people, which will include the process of having you describe, both out loud and on paper, your maiming memories, as we slowly surround you with pictures of weapons and corpses. We will measure your heart rate and other vital signs to make sure you reach your maximum. When your body reaches this heightened state of arousal in relation to maiming, the bell will ring to indicate the desired association, at which point we will clamp your eyelids open and you will view a panoramic image of a generic muddy footprint.

RING

Now you are to listen to the bell five more times, and each time it rings you will see the image of the generic muddy footprint. As this happens, you should begin to notice an increasing drive to violently confront the footprint. We will do this several times today and you will return for six more weeks of treatment.

RING RING RING RING RING

When we have finished with this series of treatments, your propensity towards violence and its new relationship with muddy footprints should successfully be triggered by the sound of a bell, anywhere, at any time.

CAN YOU USE THAT IN A SENTENCE
| HENRY HOKE

Emm Eye Ess

Um

Emm Eye Ess Ess Eye Pee Pee

Eye Pee Pee

Eye Pee Pee

Emm Eye Ess Ess Eye Pee Pee Eye Pee Pee Eye

--

In the continuing adventures, Tom and Huck stand on an otherwise empty elementary school staircase and share their first punch. They share it because Tom delivers it and Huck takes it, right in his sunken chest. Huck is impressed. He says "my solar plexus" like it truly hurt. Tom believes this, and feels the same blow.

The reason for the punch was Tom lost the spelling bee and Huck laughed.

--

What do your moms do for work? What do your dads want people to say when they walk into your house?

Huck's dad introduces Tom to sarcasm. Tom looks up and says that he's sorry he ate too many jellybeans before dinner. Huck's dad says, "well I won't spank you this time."

The boys always want a tree house, but the only time they climb to build one Huck puts his head in a hornet's nest and falls from the tree, his face swells up and Tom doesn't recognize him at school all week.

--

When the storms come they build a fort inside. Each tiny room has its own color-coding, its own vibe, hidden boom boxes pump different tunes. One of the rooms has an upside-down wicker basket as a skylight for the ceiling fan. This is where the stuffed animals live and the stuffed animals listen to mom's music. In this room, Tom has a thought. He's basically a baby so it's a baby thought, but it's that he could just die. This is the dream home. He joins Huck in the pitch dark of the thrash metal room and with a flashlight they plan a slip n slide for when the sky clears. Here in the midst of their masterpiece, Huck could grow up to become a killer or an architect, but this is the greatest thing either of them will ever do. And they did it together.

--

Tom can spit farther than Huck. Huck wants a rematch but Tom just wants to make up secret words for the next time they're in the presence of girls.

The parents don't like the two boys hanging out anymore. They tell the school to put them in separate classes.

Do you remember the last year we passed valentines? What did mine for you say?

--

Jealousy is okay if we're both jealous of each other. You can be jealous of my new two houses, my two Christmases, and I can be jealous of how much glue you can eat.

Tom and Huck draw straws stuck down in Coke cans on a canvas. Art class is the period where they can safely feel dangerous, where something impacts something something. They'll fill in the some-things later. For now Tom watches as Huck signs his drawings with an F in place of the H.

--

A dead relative drags Tom deeper south to reunite with extended family. There he meets the real evil boys, the real evil boys who ride four-wheelers through the grass on America's birthday, and who blow their own hands off with fireworks and guffaw at the stumps. Nothing fazes the real evil boys, but Tom knows they're pronouncing cicada wrong.

Nobody wants to fall asleep first.

--

When Tom goes to a party alone he fucks up and ODs and is grounded for the movie premiere of the century. Huck has the tick-ets, and plans a daring rescue. "Sneak out at quarter to midnight and I'll come for you."

Tom sneaks out his window at quarter to midnight and sits on his front porch, watching the street, waiting for Huck's headlights.

Tom sits until morning.

--

After school, Huck makes Tom drive as fast as he can to Huck's house. He wants to get there quick, not for mischief, but for Oprah. Oprah says find what you love in yourself before you try to find what you love in somebody else.

Huck says he wants to go on Oprah and champion cereal for dinner.

There's nothing nicer than a muted commercial break.

Tom asks Huck to prom, you know, as a joke. Huck asks Tom to prom, you know, to fuck with people. Neither does, neither goes. Weeks later they get to wear caps and gowns, but then the big world abducts their summer.

--

Imagine you are an adult, sleeping next to whomever, both of you in the fetal position. Spooning. It's that time, of course, a little bit night and a little bit morning. At the split second of waking, when you realize you're holding onto another person, grazing that person's back with your front, in that split second you think it's him. You recoil, from shock and pleasure and then guilt. But it's not him. It won't be him. Not in the city, not in the car, not on the other coast. Not for goddamned decades.

--

You don't know the difference between a sunroof and a moon roof, but you know that a moon roof is better.

Tom's dad calls to ask Tom a weird question. Very alone, Tom listens as his dad says "Now you can tell me honestly, I won't get mad, but were you ever in North Carolina? Driving? Because I just received a speeding ticket in the mail that has your name on it, from North Carolina." "Of course not," Tom says. "I figured," says Tom's dad, clearly disappointed.

"I imagined it might've been you and Huck," Tom's dad goes on, "I imagined you two just gunning it down the highway in a convertible, across state lines, like a joyride."

Tom imagined that too, but it didn't happen.

--

Huck is a constellation, Tom is all gazing up, can never know what Huck was ever thinking, if it ever meant as much, if he ever loved or felt the same way, if he even remembers.

Tom grounds himself in the groaning city.

Huck is a projection on the side of an express train flying by a hometown that Tom has long left behind.

A SELECTION FROM *"FLESH OF THE PEACH"*
| *HELEN MCCLORY*

She stood out on the observatory of the Empire State Building in the failing light, felt delicate and underslept, and awaited something decisive to occur. Maybe she'd be there until closing. Did they close this place? Every night the top of the building glowed different colours. Beacons for the various dread causes. And maybe out of cause-kinship, every night, all through the night, they let fools gather to acknowledge their own.

Sarah's causes? They were slimy, incriminating, broken, partial. She rummaged in her bag for a candied ginger. Sucked down on sticky fire, and squinted out across the city. I am all alone, she thought, who the fuck could aid me but me? She pulled down the sunglasses from the top of her head. That helped. You should always at least have a bit of poise. It wasn't that she particularly cared if tourists noticed she had been crying. Just that she was fond of her projections. The kind of person who went to her solitary bed in light makeup and skimpies in order to present fierce aspect. To herself, to anything in the world that might be leering in her window.

It is strange the ease in which you can enact projections. Flip down the shades and step into another life. A gilded life. It could happen, it happened. As if on cue, camera flashes crashed against her raw skin. Longhair swish. She bared her teeth for pictures taken by strangers. The milling crowd jostled her, craning towards the skyscrapers and calling out, that's the Hudson! Look, a helicopter! Happy enough. A Murmur glut passing through the channel of her body.

Sarah looked beyond the silver of the bars. It was beautiful. All the city in the early evening was lavender and greys of rare distinction, twenty miles worth of it touched by haze. After a while Sarah mumbled to the bars a prayer of falling. How to fall through a cage three metres high. She would have to shred herself. What a scene. People lingered waiting for dusk to flicker into night, others left quickly. She made tiny movements with her hands. She listened to voices detaching from the stream and threading away back inside. Are we doing this, then, she asked herself.

The question was vague because she herself was vague. It becomes a lyric in a city like this one. Sarah's lover Kennedy had just severed ties. Kennedy had been everything for a while there. A streak of lightning, against an otherwise drab sky. A rooted New England New Yorker married to a man who sounded, in his calls and written messages, limply vile. And violent, now. Out of all options which were preferable – violence done by another or the violence you do to yourself? Sarah felt she was standing on that other ragged side of love, where gravity wore thin the edges of the body. You have to ask yourself the most ridiculous questions. Do you want to live. Is your living a worthwhile act. Do you want an extra shot of caramel. Are you going to be able to pick your teeth right out of your jaw. Who the hell is keeping note, at any rate.

Sarah licked her lips and the wind chilled them. Her teeth pinched her tongue. Yes she still had lips, teeth. She still had her silky black hair, her best treasure. No jumping today. Instead, I am going to leave, she thought. She unwrapped another ginger chew, slid it in her mouth and pondered this decision. Fuck it, I ruined this whole city for myself, but I have plenty more. This is a very American thing to do.

She stared out through the bars with what she assumed was an empty expression. She turned to face the crowd in the same way. Her mother was dead back home in England, that was the other thing. Finally, after a slow war with cancer. And long after their relationship had died. The idea of going back to Cornwall to help with the estate and put on a show beside the other relatives and hangers-on made her feel unsanitary. It grubbied her.

Sarah opened and closed her fists in an effort to jog her blood pressure. She felt the problem in terms of altitude sickness or else chaffed nerves, and when she wasn't leaning on something her vision trembled. But how lucky she was, her mother had left all those millions to her. Just put it in a clean little envelope, Madam Barrister, thank you very much, like a neat towelette slipped alongside the balled-up pink knickers from last night.

She unwrapped another ginger. Sugar rush helped, fire helped. Working the wad against her back teeth, almost choking her. Two paths had emerged. One home across the pond, and another unseen in the American interior beckoning her. It was an easy choice, all considered.

TIME OF KILLING OFF SURPLUS
| GARY J SHIPLEY

His diet has not seen light or colour.
His proteins born inside a hospice suite.
And another failed attempt to settle back into the dimensions of rooms-in-general.
And they take it from him.
And they crap out toenails and eyelashes, make craven effigies of weather.
And I chew on the landscapes in my ears.
The afterbirth of a cadaver.
The scar tissue in my incubator.
Because the walls are changing colour: the old green, the white before that...
When his mouth is this cunt.
His teeth, shrapnel from exploded babies.
And my hair inscribed with negative airflow.
His offspring, organs made of tar.
Some waxwork human fruit.
When I've acquired the posture of a slug.
Cloth stuffed in place of the air in there.
The tongue a rag in a petrol bomb.
Because I feel reasons suiciding in newly isolated swarms.
When the rock is a cloud I scoured off my lung.
And I breathe solids in my sleep.
Because it's not me made meaningless by this series of emptying-outs, just always the other way round.
And the eyes going shut, and the mouth going kissing up blood.
A starved gorilla puking swallows.
And my body an impersonation of all the other bodies I see.
Like pre-chewed chicken wings squirming in gangs in lost areas of the moon.
When thought of other planets videodrome my sitting watching. The inside surfacing the only surface left.

When the door beside me fills up with maggots inside flies in the spiders in the webs in there.

When these hands are bodiless, mucking out the mouth.

And retched organs form into the shape of a reservoir, simulated in phases of being formed that way.

So many fake partitions dismantled, to be reassembled in my blindsight.

Just six boils festering on the face of God.

Just the distant drone of numerical frictions, fretted inertias, subtractions multiplying all by themselves, lost frequencies uncoiling the whine of the world.

And I baptise my smiles as baby farts.

Because the son is my son.

Even if I have to cut him down the middle to make two.

And there's a sky outside this room coloured with holes and water.

All of them together: a human swatch of burnt away fats.

Sick animals drunk on the vertigo of their pending disappearance.

And it's possible I'll ingest the witness in one.

When the contusion is still this moving thing.

Bodies fluent in their lassitude, organisms slowing to become unfixed.

When I haven't had an erection in a month.

And this is my idea for a life.

That that sky is my sky now.

And away from the screen there are stage sets of rooms, kept inside other rooms, and eyes painted over the top of eyes.

And the pack coming pissed and untoothed.

Because civilisation was pleasant once, and a frenzy then of gums.

Because the tension will peak with falsified depictions of endless one-way migrations.

Lifted up, growing, gurgling the sun, this infant cattle boy.

When already it's so: our ready acceptance of death just altitude sickness.

And the rate at which my material conditions remain the same has started to accelerate.

When life in here is all the many uncompleting circles in my ceiling.

The telescopic dead-ends of crudely opened light.

When the screen removes the room, has it sit in its void both sides of the door.

And one more abused boy is dragged to the summit to watch the sun burn out his eyes.

Because he's florescent in the feedback of his being extinguished this way.

Because I cough the thoughts out pre-numbed and half-digested.

When the fire is just one more heatless flicker of white repeated to suggest heat.

And the copying reveals what's imperceptible, while the process fails its objects by allowing them to be seen.

In the same way I once suspected birds of substituting their organs for baby food.

Because they want me to believe that reasons are medieval innocuities.

That my reasons have moved on.

That they sit behind my seeing doing things.

Collaging some clot in dead hair and shed skin to prop my watching on. This daily excavation made all puffy by my many electric self-resuscitations. As if straining at the molecular level. Which is meaningless.

And so I decide they're just five flightless birds that have found the sky inside a newborn boy imagining himself a newborn bird.

And the earth is not a nest.

Because I arrive here a thousand times a day.

And I imagine that when lava cools it concludes. That there is peace in this concluding. And that some one thing can truly end and then be done.

A SELECTION FROM "DEAR RA"
| JOHANNES GÖRANSSON

Dear Ra,

Jesse Garon is my best friend here. It may seem unfair that a child who drowned and a child who didn't know what hit him should live in hell. I'm just the devil. I don't make the rules. I make shoes out of boys and shoe-boxes out of girls. They call me "the foot," but I wish I were leather. There are no cows here, only rabbits and scaly specie, like crawfish and strychnine. Once I swallowed my friend and her scales scraped inside my chest for months. I had to build myself a cage out of gnarled objects, like a doll from a plane-crash, a shoe chewed by a dog. Here I sit all day. There's no place like it. I'm never locked out.

Dear Ra,

It smells like someone's painting my apartment. I like to smoke cigarettes when it's raining and when my brain is breaking. My dad is fat like one of those animals that live in mud! I don't like to be alone but this is ridiculous. Some people write with their fingers. I liked going to school but I couldn't stand cutting up animals. The only thing I learned was the smell of formaldehyde. The only friend I made was a nervous disorder. His hands shook like gasoline. My room is a circus. Don't run off with the zebras! Their hooves are made of cotton. You'll count the hours on your ribs. Before I was a circus director I was a museum. You can still feel the scars! Before I became the devil I fixed cars. My eyes were machine guns. Now they just squeak! I used to catch wildebeests. That's how I fed hell. That's how I tried to talk to you, but you don't like meat. You didn't think this poem was going to be about you, did you? You thought I was finished with your cigarettes. You thought I was just going to be writing about lice from now on. Nobody can fool me. I drowned already as a child. I wanted to ride straight out of hell with you. I drew up the plans when I was a kid. I drew them in the sand with my little stiff pecker. I've never used the word "pecker" before in my life! I wanted the wheels to hurt. I wanted the bags to be plastic. I wanted the animals to struggle. I wanted your thighs around my head. Cars don't work like that anymore. Cars are clean. Cities are empty. I'm the devil! I understand formaldehyde! I thought I could pick your arms, but sometimes even the circus gets eaten alive.

PROBLEM OF PLAGUE
| LAUREN HILGER

Some of the elements of life
will survive microbial disaster,
will refuse to recognize us,
will come up to the newspapers
and affect a response.

Descartes found himself in the bright blue
strong wind of the northern climate.
The erratic queen demanded he give her philosophy
at five in the morning and, calling in a cold,
he died.

On this side of enlightenment,
a bald man combs
his remaining hair for the reading.
He cannot exhale himself
into someone else's mouth. He and I

wish that fresh lemonade
sign were true. Nothing is
promised to everyone. Kant opened a door
he then closed. Still bruised where the watchface sits.
How do I get rid of miasma again? this scary beak of herbs?

stick to my bowler hat? a stick to whack your filth
away from me?
Life too near,
under the blanket, touchy with hate.
We lie in bed, hands on our stomachs like fat professors.

Still.
We are unscathed lemons.
The sky of him.
The Swiss après-ski
of this face.

Healthy and here.
The nonce. The Entstehung.
How sudden then, as I turn to swoon out, nearly, could have, felt.
What did Dostoevsky smell before
his body betrayed him? Oranges?

A SELECTION FROM "THE DEPRESSION"
| MATHIAS SVALINA

The morning after the prom the prom-king woke up still the prom-king. He went to the fast food place to get a breakfast burrito & the beaming manager wouldn't take his money: *On the house*. As he drove down Elm Street, cars pulled over to let him pass. Children waved furiously from back-seat windows. He enjoyed the attention & when his prom-reign didn't fade after days & then weeks he began to take the free coffees & sly glances for granted. Soon nothing could happen without him at the center of it, he had to deliver the news & sing for the band at each club & deliver the mail & change the minivan's axle, all while the townspeople crowded the doors, their slug noses smearing the glass, grabbing at his hands as he entered the automatic doors to the 24-hour, eternally lit Home Depot. By the end of the story the prom-king cannot remove the plastic crown from his head. He takes all his clothes off & the sash is still there. He finds a cave & he walls himself in, brick-by-brick. He grows more content, more recognizably himself as the light disappears, not trying to relax, to feel extraordinary or unafraid, refusing all that requires a design or prefix. And me? I'm the writer of blurbs. All I want is more darkness, more fun, more fish-man monsters with oranging teeth.

A SELECTION FROM "BRUJA"
| WENDY C ORTIZ

8/10/03

We swam in an above ground pool that was cavernous and deep. I shared it with other people staying at the same hotel. I held onto the concrete edges and pushed myself up and down in the water while I watched a little boy get very close to a dolphin (though someone called it a whale) that was speeding around in our midst, coming up near us then plunging into the deep again.

When the animal surfaced, it was indeed a small whale. A huge sea turtle also surfaced, so much so that I saw its entire body lunge out of the water. The little boy threw himself at its shell playfully. I got angry. He acted as though this sea turtle was a toy.

I swam around the edges of the pool looking for his parents. They were drinking champagne even though it was morning. They looked pale, groggy, overdressed. They barely paid any attention to me as I calmly suggested that they teach their son not to play rough with the animals. I swam away when I realized they weren't listening.

I was suddenly in a different pool altogether and it was shallower with no animals. There was a television up in the corner of this gym-like room. The host of a local talk show announced that they would be doing a show on 'excommunication'—which referred to excommunications from art groups.

I smiled to myself and did laps.

People around the pool began to get up and leave to go to the taping of the show. Someone from school, a woman I don't know well, called out to me, "Are you coming?" and I said, almost laughing, "I'm already an expert in being excommunicated!"

I moved from the pool to a rented room with a large bed where I reclined, channel-surfing. Ren was there. He looked older, staid, dressed conservatively. He was seducing me as usual. I couldn't get past his attire, though, and while we made the motions of foreplay, I wondered about why he had completely changed his look. I wasn't sure I liked it.

9/10/03

Everyone around me was on LSD, or 'shrooms, and there was some kind of involved game going on, with hundreds of people participating, and I saw lots of strangely folded paper with clues, the paper like college-ruled notebook paper, pen scrawls.

Young men took running leaps and scaled the sides of buildings up to three stories high before they tumbled back down onto the grass and did it again.

I got upset with someone for not explaining the elaborate game to me. I met Queena on the swing, this very intricate swing/pulley system that we used to get from floor to floor of an open-air party house several stories tall. I learned that Queena was a hardcore drug user, a piece of information that more than surprised me.

9/12/03

Stephen and I lived together, only our bedroom was my childhood bedroom. Sunlight streamed in through the blinds.

We hosted a huge party. We had hardwood floors and I liked this. I opened my closet and most of my clothes were missing, but I found this very cool dress, white and full, with one scratchy petticoat sewed into it, and the bodice had purple and pink dots.

I said to Stephen coyly, "Want me to wear this?" and he reclined across the bed grinning at me. I rubbed the bottom of the dress, the material of the petticoat, across his lips.

OFFICIAL

CCM ◗

GET OUT OF JAIL
* VOUCHER *

- -

Tear this out.

Skip that social event.

It's okay.

You don't have to go if you don't want to. Pick up
the book you just bought. Open to the first page.
You'll thank us by the third paragraph.

If friends ask why you were a no-show, show them
this voucher.

You'll be fine.

- -

We're coping.

◗

http://copingmechanisms.net/